"Don't shoot," Sean ~~said to the~~ e thug pointing a gun at them.

How could he be so calm? Deanna couldn't think straight. She doubted she could even speak, but here was Sean telling this guy how it was going to be as if he were one of Sean's hired hands.

Without waiting for permission, Sean turned, keeping his hands high. Deanna hesitated for a beat and then followed his lead, brittle pine needles crunching under her boots as she turned. The shotgun's barrel raised dead even with Sean's head, making Deanna's throat constrict. She tried to swallow, but her mouth was too dry.

"Don't move!" The guy behind the gun demanded. He sounded nervous. Scared enough to pull the trigger?

"Easy," she begged.

If they could disarm him somehow, Sean could take this guy.

Sean didn't seek out chances to prove his masculinity like some men she knew, but Deanna had seen him win a fight before.

Even staring down the barrel of a shotgun, having him next to her made Deanna feel safer.

Becky Avella grew up in Washington state with her nose in a book and her imagination in the clouds. These days she spends her time dreaming up heart-pounding fiction full of romance and faith. Becky married a real-life hero and follows him around begging him to give her material she can use in her stories. Together with their children, they make their home in the beautiful Northwest.

Books by Becky Avella

Love Inspired Suspense

Targeted
Crash Landing

CRASH LANDING

BECKY AVELLA

HARLEQUIN LOVE INSPIRED SUSPENSE

Recycling programs for this product may not exist in your area.

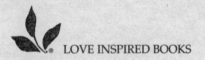

LOVE INSPIRED BOOKS

ISBN-13: 978-0-373-67825-9

Crash Landing

www.Harlequin.com

Printed in U.S.A.

I will say of the Lord, He is my refuge and my fortress: my God; in Him will I trust.
—*Psalms* 91:2

To Mom and Dad—
Always the wind beneath my wings.

This book is also dedicated to the people of Okanogan
County who faced the Carlton Complex Fire of 2014
and the Okanogan Complex Fire of 2015
with such inspiring bravery and resiliency.

Acknowledgments

This story could not have been told without the help
of pilots Michael Nitzel and Bob Sandefur,
and firefighters Dereck Bohan and Chad Sheets.

I'm so grateful for your willingness to share your
expertise with me. You can't be blamed for any mistakes
I made. Thank you for making this story stronger.

ONE

Deanna Jackson just wanted to see the sky. The tiniest sliver of blue would be enough.

The real sky was up there somewhere, hidden behind the canopy of smoke hovering above the rooflines of Main Street. It called to her to be free, to escape the doom and the stress in her airplane, but she couldn't. Although it looked like it was nearing nightfall, it was really only eleven in the morning, and Deanna was stuck indoors. Stuck being a grown-up with bills to pay.

Eerie shadows flickered through her coffee shop windows, making the inside of The Hangar feel too bright, as if its cheeriness offended the gloom outside. Occasional chunks of charred debris and ash dropped onto the sidewalks like dirty hail, a taste of what awaited the small town of Kinakane, Washington, if the wildfires bearing down on them weren't contained.

"Make that coffee extra hot, please." Sharon Grabe's hands trembled as she dug through her purse for her wallet. Sharon was one of the many refugees stranded in town awaiting word that she could return to her home, wondering if her house in Salmon Creek still stood and if her husband would get out in time. If he'd be smart enough to know his life mattered more than a building, no matter how many generations of memories that building might hold.

"What are you doing, Sharon? Put that money away," Deanna insisted.

Sharon slapped her debit card on the counter and covered it with her hand. There was no trembling now. Her resolve solid as stone, she slid the card across the counter. "Don't make me a charity case, Deanna. Not yet, anyway. I'm not ready to exchange hope for a free latte."

Deanna swallowed the lump in her throat, wishing she had more to offer, but she knew she'd despise the pity she was feeling for Sharon if it were turned in her direction.

Townspeople used to complain about a little summertime smoke in the air caused by far-off wildfires in the mountains. Now the entire Northwest appeared to be ablaze, and five separate fires hemmed them in, sucking the life out of already taxed firefighting resources.

The threat squeezed in on Deanna so tight she could hardly breathe.

She felt the flames coming, their approach rumbling through her like the vibrations of an ancient army marching on a besieged city. More and more refugees were streaming into town bringing new horror stories every day. Homes and ranches that had been in families for generations, obliterated by infernos. Old Harley Hopkins died of a heart attack because after telephone poles burned out in Scotch Creek, he had no phone service to call 911.

One way or another, it was clear Deanna wouldn't escape this fire season unscathed. Even if she didn't physically lose anything, seeing her neighbors suffering like this hurt enough.

Her grandmother's voice cut through her thoughts, snapping her focus back on more immediate concerns.

"How long do you plan to make the king of Kinakane wait for you?" Gram whispered.

Deanna's gaze landed on the tall, broad-shouldered man in the leather easy chair by the front door. Her landlord removed his Stetson and leaned forward to rest his elbows on his knees, obviously impatient with her. Deanna's stomach knotted. It wasn't just the smoke that

choked her. She was stalling, and Blake Ransford wasn't the waiting kind of man.

Blake might not be an actual king, but he
really did own most of Kinakane. He could
be overbearing, but he was her mentor, always
quick to bail her out whenever she needed it.
Because he was seven years older than she was,
it had never occurred to Deanna that Blake
might want anything more from their friend-
ship. But last night in an unguarded moment,
he'd confessed that he wanted much more than
she did.

Hot coffee sloshed over the edge of the
mug she held, scalding the back of her hand.
"Ouch!" She dropped the cup, sending a sticky
river across the counter.

Deanna waved her hand to cool it. Who
wanted this hot of coffee in July, anyway? She
reached for a clean mug to remake Sharon's
drink, but Gram's soft, wrinkled hand on her
arm stopped her.

"When are you going to get it through your
thick head that you don't have to do this all by
yourself? Get going already."

Deanna glanced at Blake. His confession had
come out of left field. She didn't know how to
feel about it, but if she let him, he could help
her.

When she laid her head on her pillow each

night, the word *bankruptcy* echoed through her mind, stealing any hope of sleep. Now there were rumors of next month's big rodeo being canceled. The whole town needed those tourist dollars, but without them Deanna would be finished. If there was no Roundup, she'd have to close The Hangar.

Blake had promised to give her some advice over lunch. Lunch was harmless enough, right? She'd just have to be honest with him.

"Fine," she huffed and surrendered her mug to Gram.

Blake stood. "Ready?"

How could she make him see she was in survival mode? Every bit of energy went into finding a way to provide for her and Gram. To keep from failing. If she said these things to him, he'd only offer her money. That's not what she wanted. She wanted to prove to herself and everyone else that she could make it on her own.

Besides, wasn't the fire threat enough stress? Were they supposed to go on a date right now and pretend that those fires weren't marching toward them?

She started to speak, but the little bell above the front door jangled in alarm. All eyes turned to watch a dark-haired cowboy rush inside. At the sight of him, Deanna's face flushed and an old pang of guilt tightened her chest.

"Sean?"

He strode toward her, passing Blake without a second glance. Deanna's mouth dropped open. Nobody ignored Blake like that.

No one except Sean Loomis, apparently.

Dressed for work in a black T-shirt and Wranglers, Sean didn't look as if he'd taken any time to spit-shine himself for town like Blake had done. It looked instead like he'd left straight from horseback. His boots were still dusty and his hair was flat on top where a baseball cap must have sat minutes earlier.

"I need to hire a pilot," Sean demanded. "It's an emergency."

Deanna closed her gaping mouth and pushed away the old high school memories. That was history; this was business.

He ran a hand through his raven hair and cocked an eyebrow. "Can you help me?"

Blake stepped beside Deanna and put a possessive hand on her elbow. "Actually, we were just leaving."

Sean balled his fists, his lips a straight, hard line. "I'm trying to save a horse, Deanna. I thought if anyone would understand that, it would be you. I'll pay you cash. More if you come with me right now."

Deanna pulled her elbow free from Blake's grip. She'd known Sean Loomis her whole life—they'd been in the same schools since kindergarten, had competed in rodeo and 4-H together—but she'd never known him to be this assertive. He looked different, too. Was he taller?

It wasn't just inches. His baby face had been replaced with a more chiseled version. The Native American features he'd inherited from his father were more recognizable than ever. How had she missed this change? She must have been blind, because this was not the skinny loner she remembered riding bareback around the rodeo grounds in high school. This was a man on a mission.

"I think she made it clear that she's not going anywhere with you today, Loomis," Blake said. "Have you looked at the sky out there? How could you think of going up in those conditions?"

"Where are we flying?" Deanna asked. The fires were far enough away for her to fly legally as long as she didn't get in the way of the fire crews. This was her business, not Blake's, and she didn't appreciate his acting so territorial.

"My ranch." Sean's shoulders slumped. "He's a new stallion—I haven't even had time to name him yet. I had him in the stables and somehow he got loose. Could have been a cougar or bear chased him up into the timberline.

I'm not sure, but I've got to find him before the fire gets to my place, and I'm running out of time. Can you help me or not?"

Blake stood up to his full height and faced her, his arms crossed. His eyes were cold, more navy blue now than cobalt. She and Sean hadn't bowed down to the king's wishes. Blake couldn't be used to that.

Deanna gnawed on her bottom lip again.

"Gram?" she called over her shoulder. "Can you cover for me?"

"Sure," Gram said.

"Wait!" Blake grabbed Deanna's arm as she passed by him. "I thought we were going to lunch."

Deanna avoided looking into his eyes. "I'm sorry, but I've got a paying customer."

Then she followed Sean out the door without looking back.

"Are you going to survive, cowboy?"

Sean exhaled and relaxed his white-knuckled grip on the door handle. He gritted his teeth. "I'm okay."

Sweat rolled down his spine. Deanna had the pilot-side window pushed open as far as it would go, and a small fan attached to the dashboard whirred at the heat. None of it did any good. It was hotter in the cramped cockpit than it had been on the ground. Shouldn't it be cooler in the clouds?

The blue-and-white Cessna dipped suddenly, and Sean's stomach nose-dived along with it. He glared at Deanna.

"Sorry." Her melodic laughter rang through his headset. "You're looking a little green, Sean."

He shifted in his seat and wiped his sweaty palms on his jeans. He was a rough-stock rider. It was common for him to ride a bull, a saddle bronc and a bareback bronc all in one night of rodeo. And during Roundup every year, he competed in the Ridge to River Run, riding a mustang straight down the side of a sharp hillside. He knew how to manage fear. But soaring through the air in a machine that felt less substantial than a breath-mint tin? That was a whole new experience.

"Can't be worse than riding a bull, can it?"

He looked down at the rugged, high desert valley below him. "Just a lot farther to fall off." He'd barely finished his sentence before they dropped elevation again. He sucked air through his teeth and glanced sideways, studying Deanna.

She was dressed in faded jeans and a cotton blouse. Practical but feminine. Just his style. But what was new? Hadn't Deanna Jackson always been just his style? It was the fact that he obviously wasn't her style that had kept them apart.

He looked away. As nice as it was to be alone with her—something he would have paid money for in high school—he had a job to do that was far more important than flirting with a pretty girl.

Her voice crackled in his headset again. She pointed out the window to his right. "There's one of the fires there—can you see it?"

Sean spotted the orange lick of flame glowing behind the foothills that housed his ranch. Plumes of menacing black smoke billowed high above the eastern horizon. Unless the winds changed or some freak snowstorm fell in the middle of July, that fire was heading for his land. Seeing it from this perspective made it all the more real. He sighed. He should be down there getting ready for it.

"We're here," Deanna said. "I'm going in closer."

Sean grabbed the binoculars at his feet and brought them to his eyes as Deanna flew low over Loomis and Callaghan Cattle Co. From this height, his home and all the outbuildings looked like tiny dollhouses.

He lifted the binoculars toward the timberline.

Somewhere hidden among those trees was the $50,000 horse he'd owned for less than a week.

Sean massaged his forehead as his gut twisted into knots once again. It seemed like it was his lot in life to be searching for the lost. The disappearance of this horse was painfully similar to another unexplainable disappearance in Sean's past, and he didn't appreciate revisiting this level of helplessness and guilt. A weight pressed against his chest as he pictured the yellowing missing-person flyer pinned to the bulletin board in his office. The corners of the paper were beginning to curl with age, marking how long the mystery of his missing father had gone unsolved.

The irony wasn't lost on Sean. It was that same poster that had driven him to spend his life savings to buy the stallion in the first place. He'd had good intentions—diversify to include more than just cattle, build a breeding business that could help pay for a better private investigator. But none of his good intentions mattered if that horse stayed lost.

Be anxious for nothing, he recalled from his Bible reading that morning. Easier said than done, but it was truth he needed all the same. Worry and guilt were getting him nowhere.

They wouldn't stop the approaching flames or help him find his horse.

They wouldn't bring Dad back, either.

Deanna sat up straight, suddenly alert. "What was that?"

She craned her neck to look over her shoulder behind them. Sean followed her gaze, goose bumps covering his arms. "Did you see the horse?"

"No." She looked back again and then flipped around to stare at Sean. "How come you have a landing strip up here?"

"We don't," Sean said.

"You do. I just saw it."

Deanna eased the plane into a turn, heading back where they had come from only moments before. "I want another look."

"I'm telling you," Sean said. "I've been over every inch of this land. I would know if we had a *runway* on our property."

"And I'm telling you, you're wrong," she argued.

Her straight, sun-bleached hair fell in front of her fine-boned shoulders as she squinted through the window. Her lips parted in concentration. Whatever it was she thought she'd seen, she was determined to find it.

But Sean wasn't paying her to go exploring.

They had one objective. Whether she approved or not, Deanna wasn't sidetracking him.

"I'll look into it later," he promised her. "Nothing matters more than finding that horse."

Deanna startled. She seemed so intent on solving this mystery it was like she'd forgotten he was still sitting there. Or was she just shocked that he'd dared to have an agenda that didn't match her own?

"You don't think this could be related?" she challenged.

"Maybe. But I don't have time for chasing maybes."

Sean winced at the harshness of his tone, but he didn't apologize. He had to make wise decisions.

"It's only an instinct," she said. "But I think we need to get down there and take a look."

Her eyes were the gray green of the sky before a thunderstorm. He'd never had the luxury of studying the flecks of yellow or the dark rims of her pupils like this. They pleaded with him to agree with her.

"Just give me the word, and I'll take us down there."

He blinked himself back to sanity. Landing a plane seemed tricky enough, but on a mountainside, using a runway she thought *might* be there? No thanks.

"Fools rush in," he said.

"No. Fools play it safe and miss out," she countered.

Sean crossed his arms. "Why would there be a runway up here? It doesn't make any sense."

Deanna nodded, "Exactly. Why? What if there are answers down there about your horse?"

She broke eye contact. "What if this has something to do with your dad?"

The question gut-punched him. The missing-person case was so cold Sheriff Johnson had stopped calling with updates years ago. After all this time, could there really be a clue? If he stopped Deanna from landing, would he get another chance to find out?

She pointed down to the ground. "There, in that draw—can you see it?"

He aimed the binoculars in the direction she indicated. "I don't know what I'm looking for."

"Trust me, it's hidden but it's there," she said. "Not a runway, necessarily, just a strip long enough to put a plane down."

He pointed the binoculars toward the meadow on the hillside and adjusted the focus. He saw the flattened, patchy grass. Then a quick flash of red between the trees caught his eye. At the edge of the meadow sat another airplane he'd never seen before. Someone was trespassing on his land.

Chills ran up his back. If Deanna hadn't pointed it out, he would never have seen it as anything other than a meadow.

"Do it," he said.

"Hold on. I won't see these landing conditions well. I'll have to adjust as we go in."

Sean found the door handle for the second time and gripped it so hard he was surprised he didn't rip it off. The buzzing motor changed pitch, and he braced himself for a rough landing.

But Deanna was a skilled pilot and performed the landing more smoothly than he'd expected. The plane taxied, decelerating, and then the propeller's spin slowed and stopped.

Sean moved to exit the plane, but Deanna stopped him. "Wait."

He stared down at her hand, soft against his arm. He shook his head slightly to clear his thoughts before his face revealed whatever remained of his schoolboy crush. He'd gotten over it. Really. His feelings for her in high school had been a distraction. There wasn't room in his life for distractions of any kind now.

She reached across him to the glove box by his knees, opened the compartment and pulled out a Glock pistol.

"Whoa." He definitely hadn't expected that. "Is that the nine or the .45?"

"The nine. It has more rounds and it fits my hand better."

She slid the Glock into her waistband. "Just in case." She covered it with her shirt and said, "Who knows who might be out there. Can't be too careful."

What could he use to defend himself? He felt the weight of his pocket contents against his thigh. Just a cell phone and a survival knife. The cell tower had burned, so the phone was useless out here. The knife was his best hope, although he'd prefer a gun. "You wouldn't happen to have two of those, would you?"

She patted his forearm and winked. "Don't worry, cowboy. I'll protect you."

Sean snorted and then followed her out of the plane. The sharp smell of wildfire burned his nostrils, and the smoke made his eyes itch. The temperature had to be in the upper nineties, if not higher. These dry, hot conditions must be miserable for the fire crews.

He hopped to the ground and looked around. He recognized where they were, of course—he'd been exploring this land from the time he could walk—but on his left stood a newly constructed storage shed he'd never seen before.

When had that been built? There was no need for storage this far out.

His neck hairs rose. "See anybody around?"

"No. No one," Deanna whispered. "Let's check out the plane."

Sean stepped to follow her, but the sliding *click, click* of a shotgun shell chambering froze him in place.

Then a voice behind him made a promise that sent ice through Sean's veins. "Take one more step, and I'll blow both your heads off."

TWO

Deanna's heart hammered against her sternum. This was her fault. She'd led Sean right into this trap, making it seem like she had his best interest at heart because she was curious. She'd even manipulated Sean with promises about his missing father. What kind of person did that?

She owed it to Sean to figure out an escape. But how?

The cool metal tucked into her waistband reminded her she had options. Her fingers twitched above her head. All she had to do was lower her hands, grab the gun and then point it at the creep behind them. Simple. That's what the gun was for. She just couldn't make herself move.

"We'll keep our hands up," Sean said, "but we're going to turn around now. Don't shoot."

How could he be so calm? Deanna couldn't think straight. She doubted she could even speak, but here was Sean telling this guy how it was going to be as if he were one of Sean's hired hands.

Without waiting for permission, Sean turned, keeping his hands high. Deanna hesitated for a beat and then followed his lead, brittle pine needles crunching under her boots as she turned. The shotgun's barrel rose dead even with Sean's head, making Deanna's throat constrict. She tried to swallow but her mouth was too dry.

"Don't move!" the guy behind the gun demanded. He sounded nervous. Scared enough to pull the trigger?

"Easy," she begged.

He looked to be in his twenties, about the same age as Deanna and Sean, but it was clear he wasn't local. He was dressed head to toe in baggy black clothes that were far too heavy for the hot weather. The muddy brown eyes under his bushy brows were hard, his mouth set in a menacing snarl. On his face was a lazy attempt at a goatee, nothing more than a thin mustache and a scraggly patch of hair on his chin.

He was just a skinny city boy. Sean had three inches' height on him and at least fifty more pounds of muscle. If they could disarm him somehow, Sean could take this guy.

Sean didn't seek out chances to prove his masculinity like some men she knew, but Deanna had seen him win a fight before. A couple of drunk, loudmouthed bullies had targeted Sean at Roundup two years ago. He'd been forced to defend himself, which he'd done swiftly and surely. They'd never messed with him again.

Even staring down the barrel of a shotgun, Deanna felt safer having him next to her. Given the right opportunity and a fair fight, she was confident that Sean would win here, too. But even if they could take the shotgun out of the picture, this guy didn't look like the type to fight fair. He seemed more of the street-fighter type. He'd probably make up for the difference in size by pulling a switchblade out of those baggy clothes.

Her eyes swept the area. They were trapped. The pilot and his gun blocked their direct path back to her plane, and there was no other escape route that she could see. If they turned and ran for the trees, he'd shoot them in the back. She wasn't even sure if he was the only man out here.

Her elbows bent slightly, and her hands lowered a few centimeters. Could she do it? How fast could she get the gun out of her waistband?

"Hands up," he commanded. She obeyed quickly, raising her arms as high as she could get them.

Her gaze passed over the wooden shed next

to the other plane. A lot of cargo could fit in there. *More cargo than one plane could hold?*

"You're the other pilot, right? Weren't you expecting us?" It was a risk, but it felt right.

She looked at Sean and tried to send him an unspoken message to follow her lead. The confused expression on his face dissipated as he caught on to the game she was playing.

Sean cleared his throat. "Yeah. Didn't anyone tell you we were coming?" His acting skills could use some work, but he'd joined her charade without missing a beat.

"Who are you?" the pilot demanded, the tip of his gun wavering. "Pritchard never said nothing about another plane."

Deanna bit back the obvious question. Pritchard? She'd never heard the name before. Time to wing it again.

"Well, he told *us*—" she amped up the annoyance in her voice "—that there'd be too much cargo for one plane. That you would need our help."

She flicked one of her raised hands in the direction of her Cessna. "We're supposed to help you transport."

The gun's tip relaxed slightly. Was he buying it?

"You didn't think we landed for a picnic, did you?" she said.

Deanna blinked rapidly. The sweat she couldn't wipe away stung her eyes. She arranged her face into what she hoped was a confident expression. This guy couldn't see fear on her face or he'd see right through her act.

Indecision danced across his features, but something else—something possessive and dark—dawned in his eyes, taking its place. His gaze traveled from Deanna's head to her feet as if he were seeing her for the first time. Heat filled her cheeks. Every part of her begged her to run from this predator, but she couldn't.

He stepped closer to Deanna, and a hissing sound escaped from Sean. Sean took a step forward. The guy waved the shotgun back at Sean's face.

"Get back!"

Deanna wouldn't want to be alone with a guy like this, but she needed to use the attraction to her advantage before Sean's cowboy code of honor got them both shot.

She added sweetness to her voice. "While we wait, can we put our arms down? Please? They're killing me."

He shuffled his feet and lowered the gun another centimeter. "Yeah. Fine. Put them down, but don't move until someone gets out here to tell me what's going on."

He locked eyes with Sean, his mouth lifting

in a cocky half smile. "I've shot a man before. I'll do it again if I need to."

Deanna froze, believing him. His eyes were so cold. He looked like a killer, like he'd follow through on that promise without a moment of guilt. She lowered her arms slowly, the gun against her stomach calling to her. *I'm here—use me.*

There was nothing to make her care about this guy, but still, he was a human being with a beating heart. She'd prepared for scenarios like this—she'd bought the gun for self-defense—but facing a real flesh-and-blood threat made her second-guess herself. It made her imagine blood and death. Even if she could get the gun out, could she pull the trigger?

Her questions took too long. Suddenly the pilot spun her, shoved the shotgun's tip between her shoulder blades and frisked her. He had her pistol in his hands before she could react to stop him.

"Hiding something?" he mocked, waving the gun in front of her face. Her fists clenched. He was too close, sharing too much of her air.

"Like you'd be out here unarmed," she snapped.

Without the gun against her belly, she was small and vulnerable. And stupid. How could she have lost the gun? Her debt to Sean had just multiplied.

"You armed?" the pilot asked Sean.

"No."

"Right," the man sneered. "Just like she wasn't."

"I'm not armed," Sean said.

"Show me," he commanded. "And don't try anything. She isn't too pretty to shoot."

Sean slowly lifted his T-shirt, revealing a tanned, muscular stomach but no gun. He repeated the process with his pant legs, lifting each side.

"Take off your boots."

Sean obeyed, pulling off his boots and shaking them out. "I'm clean."

"Turn out your pockets." Sean threw down a cell phone and a knife Deanna hadn't known he had.

The pilot kicked the knife and phone away. "Not armed, eh?"

Sean shrugged. He put his boots back on and stood back up tall, never breaking eye contact. Deanna's cheeks still burned. She'd had a gun, but she'd lost their ticket out of here by being too slow to act. She met Sean's eyes and mouthed the words *I'm sorry.*

The pilot pushed Deanna forward with the shotgun. "Walk to my plane."

When they arrived at the red Piper Arrow, he raised the shotgun to the back of her head. Deanna could feel the cold metal touching her scalp through her hair. She closed her eyes and refused to imagine the gory details of what would happen to her if that gun fired now.

"Climb into the cockpit and grab the duct tape out of the glove compartment," he directed Sean. The gun pushed harder against Deanna's head, making her stagger forward a bit. "There's two rolls. And don't forget where I've got this gun pointed."

Sean nodded and climbed in, quickly locating the tape. When he hopped back to the ground, the pilot shoved Deanna hard toward the shed. "Get up against the wall."

"Hey!" Sean yelled, stepping toward Deanna. "Not so rough!"

"Yeah, about that. Sorry about this, dude," he said and then swung the shotgun like a baseball bat, connecting with the side of Sean's head. The *thwack* of solid wood against Sean's skull made Deanna's knees buckle.

"Sean!" she screamed. Reaching out, she caught his slumping body just in time. His weight knocked her to her knees, but she slowed his fall before he hit the ground.

The pilot's hands shoved her from behind, and Sean rolled from her arms.

"On your stomach," he ordered Deanna. "And stay there or you're getting the same as he got."

Sean couldn't measure how much time passed. It could have been forever or maybe it was only seconds. Blackness condensed like a tunnel into a single point of light. He blinked his eyes, so confused. So very confused.

A woman lay on her stomach in front of him. He knew her, didn't he? Was he supposed to help her?

He tried to stand but gravity pulled at him like a magnet. He wobbled on his knees, trying not to fall.

"Stay down."

Rough hands shoved him back to the ground. A man was yelling at the girl.

Deanna. That was her name. Sean really should try to fight back. Make that guy stop yelling at her. He would. Later. After he got his head right.

No, now. Something was wrong. Deanna needed him.

Sean struggled to stand again but his body wouldn't obey. He had no more strength than a rag doll. The hands were on him again, pulling him into a seated position, pushing him against something. A dull pain throbbed against Sean's temple. He closed his eyes. He just wanted to focus. If he could only process what was happening. That's all he wanted. To stop being so confused.

Eventually, the details began to fall into place. He remembered he was with Deanna Jackson, that they had been flying. He remembered landing here and the swinging gun that had caught him by surprise. The fog was clearing from his brain but it was too late.

The pilot had tied him up, and Sean couldn't move.

THREE

The world swam in such a blur Sean quickly closed his eyes again. He tried to reach his hands up to hold his head, but his wrists were handcuffed and his arms pinned to his sides with tight duct tape. He moaned and fell sideways so he could lean against the shed wall.

Something squirmed behind him. Sean shot back up fast, releasing another wave of intense vertigo. Deanna was behind him. They were bound back-to-back with the tape securely strapping them together across their torsos. He glanced down. His legs were bound, too, just above the ankles.

"Sean? Are you awake?" Deanna sounded far away, her voice full of fear.

He started to nod but decided it was best to keep his head still. "Yeah. What happened?"

"All I had to do was reach for my gun. I had it right there but I panicked." Her voice broke. "I'm so sorry."

His chest tightened. Deanna wasn't the type to cry. Not being able to reach her to comfort her hurt worse than his head. "This is nothing, Dee. You've seen me get my bell rung worse than this riding bulls. This isn't any different than those times. I'm already feeling better."

"But he used your head like a baseball."

The throbbing inside his skull agreed with her. "Maybe. But I'll take a knock in the head over a gunshot wound any day. He didn't like being outnumbered, but he must've bought your story or he would have just shot me. That was quick thinking."

Deanna felt so tiny leaning against his back. She was a petite woman, but it had never occurred to him to think of her as small. She'd always been the golden girl, larger than life in his eyes, and far beyond his reach. In high school, she'd been like a sun with a mass of people constantly orbiting around her.

This small, sad voice wasn't hers. He wanted to squeeze her hand, but he couldn't reach it.

Sean swallowed. He needed to ask her something, but it was hard to spit out the words. Probably because he was afraid of the answer. They came out just above a whisper. "Deanna, did that guy hurt you?"

He steeled himself.

"No. I'm okay. I think he's waiting for others to show up to tell him whether or not we are who we say we are before he does anything to us."

Sean released the breath he'd held. *Thank God.* "See, you bought us time. That's good. Where'd he go?"

"He got bored, so he's rummaging through my plane."

Sean squinted toward the Cessna. "He'll be back soon."

"What do you think he's doing up here, anyway? And who's that Pritchard guy he mentioned?"

"I don't know," Sean admitted. "I'd guess he's meeting someone and whoever it is, they won't be happy to see us. This might be our only chance to get away."

"I agree, but how?" Deanna asked.

Sean flexed his chest. The tape didn't give at all. "We've got to get our hands free first. I'm going to lean forward and try to chew the tape loose around my wrists," he said. "Can you roll onto my back while I roll forward?"

They maneuvered in sync, Sean bending in half at the waist and Deanna arching backward onto the heels of her boots. Barely reaching his wrists, Sean bit at the gray tape but it was bound several times around and was too thick to chew through. He'd break through eventually, but it would take too long. He sat up slowly, easing Deanna back down behind him.

"I need something to saw with," he said.

And to stop being so dizzy. That would help.

He reached for a stick, but it was so far out of reach he almost knocked them both onto their sides trying to stretch to it. This wasn't working. He needed a plan, but it was still hard to think straight. Man, his head hurt.

Sean's back was warm where Deanna leaned against him. The pilot might not have hurt her yet, but there was no denying that hungry look Sean had seen in his eyes. He would hurt her if he got a chance. Sean needed to get her to safety, but he couldn't move.

Defeated by a city boy and a roll of duct tape. It was humiliating.

He pulled hard against the tape again, but it didn't loosen any more than it had the last time. He closed his eyes. *God, I don't know what to do. Show me how to get her out of here.*

"Got any ideas?" he asked Deanna.

Her head rocked against his back. "No. But I think you're right—we need to get our hands free first."

Sean stared at his feet. Maybe he could rub his wrists against the edges of his cowboy boots and break the tape. But that would be as slow as trying to chew through it.

"Wait." Sean sat up straight. "What kind of boots are you wearing?"

"Ropers."

"Lace-ups?"

"Yeah, why?"

He had an idea, and it just might work. "If you lean forward, could you reach your laces?"

"Probably."

Her laces should be thick enough to get some good friction. "Unlace one just enough to get it up to your mouth. If you can bite down on it and pull it tight enough, it'll give you something to saw against the tape. Can you do it?"

"I'll try." She folded over in half and followed his instructions. He tried to keep his weight off her. "Got it," she mumbled. She sat up and he rolled back.

"Okay, now, keep it really tight."

The desire to be free pulsed through him. It was so hard to sit still, to be helpless like this. He could feel the rocking motion behind him as Deanna slid her wrist up and down the boot-lace. "You gotta hurry."

"Almost got it," she said. There was a manic tone to her voice. Her enthusiasm was contagious. "It worked! My hands are loose!"

"Good," he said. "Now your ankles."

"There!"

The sound of ripping duct tape that hit his

ears might possibly have been the most beautiful sound he'd ever heard. His idea was working. He could almost taste freedom. But in the distance, the pilot jumped down from the plane.

"He's coming, Deanna. You've got to hustle."

"Almost done…"

Hurry!

And then he felt it. The tape around their torsos was loosening. He reached for Deanna and covered her hand, stopping her before she got too zealous ripping the tape off them. "Wait. Go really slow. We need him to think we're still tied up."

They helped each other pull it off as nonchalantly as possible. When they got it all off, Sean mashed the spent tape into a ball. They were free.

"For this to work, we've got to surprise him," he said. "I'll jump him as soon as he's close enough."

"He's still got the shotgun," Deanna said. "And he's got my pistol and your knife."

"What else can I do? If we go running now, he'll shoot us for sure. And if we wait any longer, whoever he's working with will get here and he'll know we were lying. Either way, we end up shot."

Knowing they were actually free and still not being able to act on it was its own form of torture. Sean kept his eyes on the man ambling toward them, trying to calculate when he should make his move. How close should he let the other guy get before he attacked?

Somehow Sean would need to leap from a sitting position and strike before the guy could raise his shotgun and shoot. Or worse, grab the knife and stab Sean. He shuddered. Knives were ugly business.

Deanna's breaths were shallow and getting more frequent behind him. His fingers found hers behind him, and he squeezed. The blurry vision, the pain in his head, it would all have to be ignored. He was getting Deanna out of here. Impossible odds or not.

"Get ready," he whispered.

With each step the guy took toward him, Sean prepared to jump. The pilot was getting closer to them. Could he see the tape was gone yet? Sean forced himself to relax, to look bored. *Just a little bit closer, closer. Now!*

Sean sprang from his spot, scrambling to get his body upright fast enough to have an advantage. Diving forward, he tackled the pilot like he would a calf for branding. They hit the ground hard.

Sean was on top. He'd had the element of surprise he wanted, but the pilot was scrappy and strong and recovered quickly.

The gun fired, the blast ringing in Sean's ears, but he wasn't too deaf to hear Deanna screaming. Was she hit?

His heart pounded as he wrestled and grappled with the man struggling beneath him. Sean fought to keep the shotgun pinned to the ground without letting the man slip out from under him. He ducked to avoid a head butt, and the pilot's head connected with his shoulder instead. Sean needed to gain control of the shotgun before he got his face blown off. He shoved his right forearm across the pilot's neck, pressing hard on his windpipe. The man's face was purple, but he hadn't stopped fighting.

Sean caught sight of Deanna in his peripheral vision. "Run for the plane," he panted.

"Not without you!"

Her arms raised above her head and he saw she held a large stone. She dropped her hands fast and *crack*. Sean winced at the sound of stone against skull, but she'd done it. The fight was over instantly as the pilot's writhing body went completely slack.

Bile burned Deanna's throat. She covered her face with her hands, hearing again that horrible sound. Had she killed him?

Sean's larger hands covered hers. They were warm and gentle as he peeled her hands away from her face. He placed the pistol she'd lost into her right palm. Then he closed her fingers around it. She kept her eyes squeezed shut. If she'd just killed that guy, she didn't want to see it.

"You did the right thing," Sean said, his voice kind. "I need you to open your eyes so you can help me with him before he wakes up."

Her eyes popped open. "He's not dead?"

Sean chuckled. "No. He'll have a nasty headache, but he's alive." Sean rubbed his own head. "For some reason, I don't feel much sympathy. Can you do something to ground his plane? I don't want him flying away before I can get the sheriff out here."

"I'll need your knife."

Sean knelt beside the groaning man and retrieved his knife and his cell phone. "Hurts, doesn't it, buddy?" Then he handed Deanna the knife and said, "Make sure he's stuck here."

As Sean worked on tying up the pilot with the remaining duct tape, Deanna jogged for the Arrow. First she punctured each tire with Sean's knife. Even on a paved runway, a pilot would need tires to take off. Without them, on this uneven ground and grass, takeoff would be impossible. But just to make sure he was truly grounded, she located the magneto line to the engine and sliced it at each end, then pocketed the cable. She surveyed her work. Satisfied, she rejoined Sean.

"That will have to do for now," he said, tossing the empty tape roll against the shed. "It's not tight enough but we're out of tape."

"Well, even if he gets out of the tape, I guarantee that airplane of his isn't going anywhere soon."

"Good work," Sean said, then returned to searching the pilot. "Let's see what we can find out about our friend here."

"That he's up to no good?" Deanna scoffed.

Sean pulled out a wallet and then an ID card. "Hmm… Nathan Reid from…" Sean looked again at the card. "Nathan Reid from Vancouver."

He tossed the wallet on the ground but pocketed the card. "Here you go, *dude*." he said. "I'll keep your ID so I can bring Sheriff Johnson a little souvenir." Then he grabbed the hard-won shotgun and stood up.

"He's Canadian?" Deanna asked.

Sean nodded. "You're a little south of your border, Nathan. What are you doing trespassing on my land?" The pilot said nothing.

A twig snapped somewhere in the distance, and Deanna jumped, her eyes scanning the meadow.

"Let's get out of here," she whispered, stepping in the direction of her plane, but Sean held back.

"What's the matter?" she asked.

Sean's jaw twitched. "I can't leave until I get some answers."

The hovering shroud of smoky haze contributed to the scary-movie feel, and Deanna's unease was growing by the second.

"Let's go," she begged. "He's coming to, and he said he was meeting people here."

"That's the problem," Sean said, pointing at the plane. "I still don't know what they are up to or who else is involved. It's like you said in the air—this is my land and I should know what's happening on it."

Without waiting for her okay, Sean turned and walked back toward the shed.

"This is nuts!" She fumed, but she jogged after him.

"As nuts as landing in the first place?" he called over his shoulder. "Weren't you the one who promised me some answers?"

"It might be my fault that we're here to begin with, but it's your fault we are *still* here," she said. Sean didn't stop.

She grabbed his arm to stop him. "Would you wait?"

Sean spun to face her, jerking away from her grip. "I can't," he said.

Deanna stepped back, stunned by the need in his eyes.

"You have no idea what it's like not to know," he said, his voice rough with suppressed emotion.

His mahogany eyes were dry of any tears, but the naked vulnerability she saw in them made her own eyes fill. Her dad had always been an absent playboy. He loved his airplanes and the Alaskan wilderness more than he'd ever loved her. But as messed up as their relationship was, at least she knew he was alive. He called her a couple times a year to fill her in on what he was up to and where he was living.

Sean hadn't heard his father's voice in six years. He'd been a junior in high school the morning that Mel Loomis got up from the breakfast table and left their house, never to be seen again. What would it be like to have your father vanish without a single clue? It had all happened so long ago Deanna had forgotten about it until it had occurred to her as a means to get Sean to let her land the plane. Of course his son would never forget. For Sean, there would never be a break from the wondering.

"It's not like I expected to find *him* here," Sean said. "We've already had a funeral. At this point in my life, I just want to know what happened."

Her need for self-preservation wrestled with her empathy.

"Okay," she conceded. "We have to hurry."

He didn't say anything, but the gratitude was written all over his face. He turned, and she followed him to the shed, but there were no windows to see inside, and a dead bolt kept them from opening the door. Deanna tugged at it. "It's locked."

"Step back," Sean said. He kicked the door hard. There was a sound of splintering wood, but the door held fast. He continued to side-kick it with his boot until the wood frame busted and the door swung wide open.

He grinned. "There—it's not locked anymore."

"I like your style, Loomis."

Once they were inside, it took a moment for her eyes to adjust to the dim interior. When she could see, she saw stacks of leather athletic bags and wooden crates.

"Are those sports bags?"

"Hockey, I think," Sean said.

"Do you know anyone around here who plays hockey?"

Sean's forehead creased. "No, I don't."

"Me neither. Especially not in July. What do you think is in them?"

"I'm not sure I want to know." Sean grabbed

the nearest one and unzipped it. He sucked in his breath, recoiling from the bag as if it were a rattlesnake that might strike. His hands went to the top of his head. "No, no, no, no."

Deanna crouched to look. The bag was stuffed to capacity with gallon-sized baggies containing a sugar-like substance secured in bundles with duct tape.

"Oh, wow," she whispered.

Sean grabbed another bag from a different pile. He unzipped it slowly. Deanna held on to his free arm and peered around him. She was afraid to look. It, too, was full of baggies, but these contained white pills. A third bag held green plants.

Deanna grabbed a crowbar off the floor. The crate lid whined as she pried it open. Tossing the large piece of wood aside, she looked inside the box and gasped.

"Sean, this is bad."

There were enough automatic weapons and magazines inside the crate for a small army. Sean and Deanna stood side by side, completely still for several heartbeats, just staring. Deanna had never seen anything like this. She dropped the crowbar to the ground without bothering to put the lid back on the crate.

"Can we go now?" she whispered. Her question was drowned out by the rumble of approaching diesel engines and the crunch of gravel under tires outside the shed.

Even in the dim interior, Deanna could see Sean's pupils expand. "Deanna?"

"Yes?" she choked out.

"Run."

FOUR

Bullets zinged around Sean as he sprinted for Deanna's plane. He was only yards ahead of the pursuing men behind him, and they were catching up quickly. Midstride, Sean turned and used the pilot's shotgun to send a warning shot at the closest man. As he pulled the trigger, recognition dawned. His pursuer was Rex Turner.

Rex owned the Wagon Wheel restaurant on Main Street in Kinakane. He was a tall man with a shiny bald head, a big belly and an even bigger smile. Sean's bullet missed, and clods of earth exploded at Rex's feet. Rex wasn't smiling today.

How many more of the men behind him would Sean recognize? Were there others he considered friends or acquaintances, men he'd done business with, who were now determined to kill him because he knew too much?

Deep guttural shouts and revving truck engines clashed with the high-pitched pinging of the bullets spitting up dirt and grass around Sean's feet, urging him forward. Some of the men had turned back for their vehicles and would reach them soon.

His lungs burned from the smoky air he inhaled and from the sheer exertion required to stay ahead of the men, their bullets and their quickly approaching trucks. He worried Deanna wouldn't be able to keep up, but she was light and fast, and she didn't miss a step.

"Don't stop running until we're in the plane," he called to her. "Keep moving no matter what. It's harder to hit a moving target."

"You're going to have to cover for me while I get the engine going," Deanna huffed. She scrambled up the plane and into the cockpit. Bullets hit the wing above her, narrowly missing her. Sean ran to his side of the plane and climbed in, using the open door as a shield.

"I'll cover you," he panted. "You worry about getting us in the air."

Deanna checked to make sure the fuel switch on the floor was on and then gave the prime a few shots. She eased the throttle partway in and then reached for the key. Her hands were shaking so violently it was hard to turn the ignition.

"Come on, come on, come on," she pleaded.

Sean kept the door open as a barrier between him and the advancing men. He bobbed up and down, answering each of their shots with shots of his own. The closest man reached the plane and was grasping for Deanna's door handle when the engine sputtered to life.

"Sean," she yelled. "Get this guy off me."

Deanna leaned forward, while Sean reached across her back, sticking the butt of the shotgun through the open window. He slammed it hard into the man's nose. The man rolled away from the moving plane, bleeding but still alive.

"That was Greg Martin," Sean said. She heard the shock in his voice, but there was no time to stop and process who was out there shooting at them.

"Time to go!" she shouted.

Deanna pushed the throttle all the way in, watching the airspeed indicator come to life. Sean fell back into his own seat, slamming his door closed.

"Come on, baby, faster," she implored the plane as it rolled down the meadow. The seconds it took to gain speed felt like months. Sean didn't say a word; his eyes were closed, his lips moving. Praying?

She used to pray all the time before her dad put the kibosh on it and convinced her it was useless. Gram was tight with God. Deanna suspected Gram spent countless hours on her knees praying for her backslidden granddaughter, but Deanna had made a decision a long time ago that she'd rely on no one but herself. Hopefully, Sean's prayers would be enough for both of them.

They gained speed, and the nose of the plane tipped up, until finally, gravity pressed against her chest. A hot breeze from the open window on her left tickled her cheek. She held her breath as they continued climbing.

Sean's eyes opened. "You did it," he said and hit the ceiling in joy. "Deanna Jackson," he chuckled, "you are amazing. I thought that was the end down there."

"Not just me. You were amazing, too. I thought we were finished," she admitted. Her voice sounded small in her headset.

Sean had fixed the mess that she had made. She might have gotten the plane off the ground, but she was still deep in his debt. She could now add him to the long list of people she owed something.

She couldn't join in his celebrating yet. Too many unknowns still needled her. So many things to sort through, like "What do we do next?" She'd celebrate when they were on the ground at the airport and far away from this madness. Even then they wouldn't be safe.

Yes, they'd gotten in the air, but those men could find them easily in a town as small as Kinakane. Where could they hide?

Deanna frowned at the instrument panel. Both the right and left fuel gauges were dropping, fast enough to make her nervous. Kinakane's airport was too rural for a traffic control tower. And if she put a Mayday out on the radio, that pilot in the meadow would be able to hear it and tell the men chasing them of their exact location.

They were on their own.

"I've got to head back for the airport," Deanna said. "I'm sorry."

"It's okay." He rested his head back. "We've had enough excitement for one day."

"Yeah, me and my brilliant ideas." Why wasn't he yelling and accusing her of almost getting him killed? "I hope you don't think I expect you to still pay me for this disaster."

"No, it's okay. I'm grateful," he said, looking out the window. "If it weren't for you, that could still be going on behind my back. I needed to know."

She sighed. Instead of blaming her, he was thanking her. Sean had always been such a good guy, even when he was a little kid. If you thought Sean, you thought nice. No one would ever say that about her, that was for sure.

"Maybe it would be better not to know. You know, ignorance is bliss and all that."

His Adam's apple bobbed. "You gave me a new lead to look into with Dad. I haven't had one in years. I can't wrap my head around him being involved in anything illegal. But what do I know? I thought he wasn't the type to ever leave us, either."

"Hopefully, this has nothing to do with him," she said.

"Hopefully," he agreed wistfully. "But I'd rather have the truth hurt than not know anything at all."

Sean exhaled, his mind racing. He sorted everything that had happened into categories and tried to prioritize what to think about first. One thought kept rising to the surface, demanding that he think about it even if it hurt. Was his family involved in this in any way? Was it just coincidence that they were using Loomis-Callaghan land, or was Sean a fool who'd been intentionally kept in the dark?

And who were the others he was referring to, anyway? "Did you recognize anyone?" he asked Deanna.

"A few. I saw Rex Turner," she said, frowning. "Our businesses are steps away from each other. I see him every day, and I eat my lunch at the Wagon Wheel a couple times a week at least. He's always been so nice to me."

Sean nodded. "And I think I broke Greg's nose."

"I can't imagine Greg being involved in this. At least, I don't want to imagine it."

"Me neither."

Greg Martin was one of their former classmates. He wasn't someone either of them would have called a close friend, but definitely more than an acquaintance. Another twelve-year vet who'd started kindergarten with them. In school, Greg was the clown, the guy everyone liked because he made people laugh.

"I bought a fishing license from him at the hardware store last week," Sean said. "I've been laughing all week at a joke he told me. I never would have guessed this."

"I'm afraid we're going to be finding out a lot more people we'd never expect are in on this," Deanna said. "I wish I could unknow all this. If I could go back, I'd never land in that meadow."

There had been something else Deanna saw down there that Sean should know, but he wasn't going to like it. She cleared her throat, choosing her words carefully.

"You're pretty tight with Sheriff Johnson, right?" she asked.

"Jim's one of my best friends," Sean said. "Why?"

"I saw the sheriff's department decal on one of the trucks down there."

She added quickly, "I didn't see the sheriff. It just seemed strange that one of their vehicles would be anywhere near there."

"Maybe they're making an arrest," Sean said.

"Wouldn't that be nice," she mumbled unconvinced, but her attention was back on the fuel situation. It was dropping rapidly.

"Uh, this isn't looking good..."

Before she could say more, the noisy buzz of the engine went dead quiet. A small cry of alarm escaped her lips.

"What just happened?" Sean asked, his voice too loud against the silence.

Deanna shook her head. Her vocal cords rebelled, as if speaking it aloud would make the situation more real than it already was. She swallowed. She was the pilot. It was imperative that she keep her cool.

"Tighten your seat belt, Sean."

His frightened gaze met hers.

"The fuel tanks in the wings must have been hit by the bullets," she explained.

"Are you telling me we have no fuel?"

Deanna closed her eyes briefly, then forced herself to admit it. "We have no fuel and no working engine, either."

She wished she and God were on better terms. *Help me.* It was all she knew to say. "You're a religious man, right?"

"Religious isn't exactly how I'd define it, but I guess you could say that."

"Then I recommend you start praying."

"Are we crashing?" He asked, his ever-steady voice finally wavering.

"No. We are not *crashing*," Deanna insisted. "But get ready, because we are going down for an off-airport landing."

"A what?"

She pointed out the window. "See that alfalfa field?"

"Yes. I own it."

"Well, now it's our new airport."

"Are you kidding me?"

"I wish I was." She met his gaze again. "Brace yourself."

FIVE

A tangible silence sat between Deanna and Sean like another passenger as the plane glided noiselessly toward the ground. Sean prayed but kept his eyes wide open. If death was near, he wanted to see it coming. Would Dad be waiting for him on the other side?

Deanna aimed for the field below. For the second time in a day, she would be landing on Loomis land. And for the second time that day, Sean wondered if he would survive it when she did.

He'd plowed and planted this field himself. This alfalfa would become the hay they needed to feed livestock during the long winter months ahead when grazing wouldn't be an option. The plants were nearly ready for second cutting. How much damage to his crops were they about to do? Would he be alive to even care, or had all that work last spring been simply the preparation of his own grave?

The twenty-acre field sat atop a plateau and wrapped around a brush-filled ravine that was too steep to farm. Somehow Deanna would need to land in the impossibly narrow strip between the sprinkler lines on the left and the timberline on the right without hitting the ravine.

At the far end of the field, Uncle Paul's farmhouse sat tall and white, the only spectator to the event. Sean's breathing shallowed as helplessness enveloped him. He watched the ground and the possibility of death come closer and closer.

Sean had always been a doer. He preferred keeping his ducks neatly in a row so life couldn't surprise him. He hated surprises. But life had a mind of its own and seemed to enjoy humbling him. Live or die here, it wasn't his call. Sean could do nothing but trust God and the skill He'd given Deanna.

In the final moments of descent, Deanna barked orders. "Get your seat up and make sure your belt is tight. This is going to sound crazy, but when I get close to the ground, I want you to open your door."

"What?"

"You won't fall out. Trust your seat belt. If the cockpit gets crunched on impact, the doors could get jammed shut. Plus, we might need to jump out fast." She pointed behind her seat. "See that backpack? I've got an old jacket in there. I need you to use it to cover up the latch so the door can't swing back and close itself again."

If he didn't worry that arguing with her would distract her, he would say more. It was counterintuitive to open his door when they were about to crash. But she was the pilot, and she knew best, so he kept his mouth shut and followed her instructions. *Lord, please help us live through this.*

The field came at them fast. What would the moment of touchdown feel like? The alfalfa looked like green grass and stood a foot to a foot and a half tall. It appeared lush and soft, level even, but it only hid how uneven and rock hard the ground would be underneath it. Would there be an explosion when they hit the ground or would pieces of the plane—and pieces of them—scatter? They needed a smooth, paved airport runway. He'd even choose the steep mountainside landing strip they'd just used over this bumpy, narrow slot of hay.

"Do it now," Deanna instructed. "Open your door."

Fighting every instinct, Sean pressed open the passenger door, revealing the speeding ground below, and flung the jacket over the door latch.

"Watch out for the irrigation circles," he hollered.

"I see them," Deanna said between clenched teeth.

Sean wanted to yell "Pause" or "Wait" or "I'm not ready." All would be useless. The ground kept coming closer and closer, and then impact. Hitting hard, the plane bounced across the rutted ground, flattening surrounding plants. The plane's wing clipped the closest irrigation line, sending the aluminum structure flying. The complaining sound of breaking metal hit Sean's ears. Was that the sprinkler line or pieces of the plane busting up? His body rocked and rolled with the bucking airplane. It was like riding a bull. Hold on for the eight seconds and then he'd be able to get out and kiss the ground.

The field wasn't an airport and no one could have ever imagined that it would be used as one, but at least the space ahead was all clear. Deanna had touched down on the open strip and now nothing hindered their progress—no trees, no houses closer than Uncle Paul's in the distance, not even a tractor got in their way.

They would survive.

As the plane decelerated, then slowed and then stopped, they sat still, gulping deep breaths.

"You alive?" Deanna asked, her eyes closed.

Sean patted down his arms and legs, opened and closed his hands. Did everything still work?

"Yeah. Are you?"

"Well, I'm talking, so I must be." Deanna leaned her forehead against the instrument panel, continuing to suck in ragged inhales. Her hands were shaking.

Sean put one of her shaking hands between his larger ones. "You did it again, Deanna." He squeezed, trying to express his gratitude and his admiration of her. "It's going to be a long time before I fly in anything smaller than a 747. But if I do, I want you to be my pilot."

She lifted her head and offered him a wavering smile. "This baby won't be going anywhere anytime soon." Then she moaned. "I don't want to go out there and see the damage to my plane."

"Well, I don't want to see the damage you did to my hay crop, either," Sean said, fake-punching her on the arm. "I'll send you the bill."

The joke fell flat. "Hey." He stretched his arm around her for a quick side hug. "It's going to be okay."

"I know that. Just give me a minute to believe it."

"I wish I had a minute to give you, but we've got to get moving. We were recognized back there and with that many men, they've spread out. They might've even seen us land here."

"Well, we can't fly away. We have no fuel, and I'm sure the plane is too beat up."

Sean doubted she could get *him* back in the air anyway, but he didn't admit it aloud.

Deanna added, "She'll have to sit in your field awhile until I can come back for her. I'm sorry."

He pointed toward the distant farmhouse. "That's my uncle's place. He's probably not home, but we can borrow a vehicle and try his landline."

The door to the farmhouse wasn't locked. It never was. As they entered the kitchen, Sean grimaced at the mess but his stomach growled. He had missed breakfast with Uncle Paul and the crew this morning, and it looked like he'd missed a feast.

Remains of the hearty morning meal were scattered everywhere. Pans, now white from the cooled grease of goose sausage and fried eggs, sat unmoved on the stove. Heavy-duty paper plates—Uncle Paul's idea of fine china— littered the rickety oak table, while crumbs and buttered knives from hastily made toast decorated the countertop. The crew had eaten well this morning.

"Uncle Paul, you here?" Sean called, but he knew his uncle was out working. Hopefully, getting the last of the cattle rounded up. Something Sean should be helping them with.

Despite how desperate he was to get Deanna back to town in one piece, there was something about this place that made him smile. He spent more time in this kitchen than in the one in his own house because Uncle Paul was a better cook.

After his father disappeared and then Uncle Paul's marriage failed shortly after, Paul had thrown himself all the more into being there for Sean. Uncle Paul, Sean and Sean's mother had leaned on each other hard during those early years, supporting each other through their grief. Uncle Paul had become the mentor and father figure Sean had needed. They'd had plenty of heart-to-hearts sitting at that oak table drinking coffee.

Deanna stood by the kitchen door waiting, reminding Sean there wasn't time for reminiscing like this.

"Sorry about the mess," Sean apologized. "Uncle Paul can cook like no one you've ever known, but he's allergic to cleaning."

Sean lifted the ancient wall-mounted phone—

probably the last left in the county—and listened for a dial tone. Nothing.

"Wish my cell worked," he said, placing the heavy receiver back into its cradle. "We've never had dependable service up here as it is, but now cell, internet, landlines, they're all gone. We've been cut off for two days."

"Service has been patchy in town, too," Deanna said. "Depending on where you're at. Some parts of town have the newer phone lines buried underground. We should be able to find a phone to use once we get back to town."

Pawing through the junk drawer under the phone, Sean found the key ring he was looking for. "Follow me."

He led Deanna to the detached building at the end of the short breezeway outside the kitchen and shouldered open the old door, releasing the garage's signature scent of diesel fuel and WD-40 spray. He reached inside and slapped around for the light switch on the interior wall.

Light flooded the small space. He kicked an empty coffee can out of his way and ushered Deanna inside, waving his hand at the rusted Ford pickup parked in front of them.

"It ain't pretty, but it should get us back to town," he said.

"I'm not picky," Deanna said.

The truck was ancient. It had been old in 1970. They only used it for work around the ranch, but it was transportation, and they had to get back to town somehow. Hopefully, it wouldn't die on them before they got there. Sean wrenched open the whining metal passenger door.

"Your chariot awaits," he said to Deanna with a slight bow.

She rolled her eyes. "You mean the Beast awaits."

"I thought you said you weren't picky."

He walked around to his own side and was about to slide into the driver's seat when a familiar noise stopped him. Diesel engines, slamming doors, angry voices. His stomach sank to the floor.

Sean ran to the filmy window and peered out.

Deanna opened her door. "What's going..."

"Shh, they found us," he whispered.

Out the window, he watched the first truck pull up into the driveway. Rex Turner, along with the pilot and one other guy Sean didn't recognize, exited the truck, their weapons raised. Sean wondered how long they'd left Nathan Reid in that duct tape before they freed him. Or had he figured out how to get out of it himself?

The men in the meadow must have split up into search groups, and this group had been assigned his uncle's place. Sean was glad he wasn't facing all those men at once, but fighting Nathan Reid the first time around had been hard enough. Now Reid had two other men to back him up, and they were all armed.

"See 'em anywhere?" Rex's muffled voice asked. He stepped into Sean's line of sight. Rex seemed to be in charge of the small group.

"Not yet," Reid answered him.

"What do we do when we find them?" asked the third man.

"We leave no witnesses," Turner answered.

His voice lowered in volume, making it more difficult for Sean to hear through the garage walls. But it was the last part he heard that mattered.

"You find them," Turner commanded. "You shoot them. It's that simple."

Deanna groaned softly. She and Sean had escaped one cage today only to find themselves in another one.

She rubbed her eyes with the palm of her hand. It had been only the span of an afternoon, but she was battle weary, tired of fighting to stay alive. How good would it feel to be back in Kinakane with Gram making coffee, with nothing bigger to worry about than money and Blake. The things that had weighed her down back at The Hangar earlier today seemed so trivial now. Bankruptcy didn't seem that scary anymore. Even the fires seemed farther away. Being shot at had a way of putting life back into proper perspective.

There had to be some way to let someone know what was happening to them. But there wasn't. Without phones, they couldn't even dial 911. She thought of Harley Hopkins and how helpless and panicked he must have felt out in Scotch Creek when he was having his heart attack, unable to call for help.

No superhero or police officer was going to come crashing in to save the day here, either. Their only hope was themselves.

Wasn't that true about life in general anyway? She was responsible for fixing her own messes. This mess just happened to have higher stakes than she was used to. It was bigger than she knew how to fix.

Her dad had tried to drill that lesson into her. "You need to have the skills to take care of yourself," he told her. "It's a dog-eat-dog world, and if you are going to survive in it, you have to look out for number one."

He might be the king of clichés, but he'd gotten his point across. And when she was only five years old, he gave her plenty of practice at being independent. He was tired of Kinakane and restless. Alaska called to him, as he put it. When the right job offer finally came through, he left her with Gram.

"It's just a job, Dee-girl. I'll be back soon," he promised. He kept up the pretense for about a year, sending her scenic postcards of the Alaskan wilderness with even more promises, "Looking at all this beauty reminds me of my beautiful girl. I'll be home soon, sweetheart."

But "soon" never came, and she'd quickly learned that he was right. She couldn't count on anyone but herself. She squared her shoulders. She would not be a damsel in distress here, either. Time to save herself.

Sean scratched the side of his head. "We need a plan."

"No, we need to get out of here."

"I know, but as soon as I open this garage door, they'll be on us."

"We can make all the plans we want, but it's time to choose. Sit in here and wait or take charge." She put her hands on her hips and tried to stand taller. "We need to take the power back," she said. "Otherwise we might as well go out there and hand ourselves over now."

Sean's eyes narrowed. "That's all good in theory. But you still haven't given me anything we can act on. They've got orders to silence us. They'll shoot first and ask questions later."

The shotgun that Sean took off Nathan Reid had been left behind inside his uncle's house. Without any shells, it wasn't worth lugging around, but Deanna still had her Glock, and she'd reloaded it before they left the airplane. She had about eight rounds. Was that enough to shoot their way out in a blaze of glory?

The walls hiding them from the armed men were thin and uninsulated. She could hear them coming closer. Her gaze jerked over to the truck. "What if we don't open the garage door at all?"

"You mean stay in here?" Sean spun around like he was playing a game of hide-and-seek, looking for the best hiding spot.

"That's not what I meant," she said. "What if…" She hesitated. This was action-movie, stuntman-type stuff she was thinking up. "What if we gun the truck and bust through the garage door?"

Sean blinked at her, the expression on his face dumbfounded. He probably thought she was insane. But he'd been thinking that all day.

"What?" she challenged. He wasn't coming up with any better ideas. "You have to admit it would give us that element of surprise you're always talking about."

A slow smile spread across his tan face, softening the chiseled stone. He really did have an amazing smile.

"You are certifiable, you know that?" Sean said.

"You've told me that a couple times today. Looks to me like doing something crazy is our only option."

She patted the truck's hood gently. "You're not afraid of letting this beast get a few scrapes, are you?" she whispered.

"Get in," Sean said.

Deanna settled into her seat, easing the truck door shut as quietly as she could.

Sean chuckled softly. "What is it you like to say? Hold on? Get ready? Oh, I know." He winked. "*Brace yourself*, Deanna. This might be a bumpy ride."

She rolled her eyes. "Very funny. You know there are guys out there with guns that want to kill us, right? You could get going anytime now."

Sean pushed the key into the ignition and turned a satisfied smirk toward her. "It's just nice to be in the driver's seat for once."

"Don't get used to it, cowboy." Deanna stared at the solid wall in front of them. She did not like being in the passenger seat like this. Her idea had felt more right in theory than it did in actual execution.

"Oh man. You were right. This really is nuts," she whispered.

"Nah, I prefer to think of it as being brave," Sean whispered back. "Ready?"

No, but she nodded anyway. The engine growled a few sleepy grumbles before it finally roared to life.

"Here we go!" Sean hollered, slamming his boot against the accelerator.

Deanna jerked backward, held hard against the ripped upholstery as the truck lurched forward, punching a hole through the old garage door. Pieces of broken wood and splinters flew around them as the old Ford broke free. It was easier than she'd thought, like a football team running through a butcher-paper sign before a high school game.

The shocked expressions on the men's faces probably mirrored her own. Rex Turner had approximately two seconds to dive out of their way to avoid getting run over. Profanity rang through the air as the three men scrambled to start the pursuit.

"Yee haw!" Deanna yelled. But then a bullet connected with the passenger-side mirror, and the thrill evaporated instantly. Glass shards exploded, leaving a hole that went straight through the mirror's metal backing. Deanna screamed and slid down in her seat. If there was any remaining doubt in her mind that they were still in danger, it was gone now. Only a slight move to the left and that bullet could have blasted through her head instead.

SIX

As they bumped along the rutted dirt road, Sean worked to stay ahead of the constant volley of bullets. He floored the accelerator, but the old truck had sat idle for too long. Its engine only whined at being pushed so hard. There might not even be enough gas in the tank to make it back to town.

His stomach flipped as Deanna hung out the side window and shot back. She shouldn't be so exposed. He grabbed her shirt's hem and tugged her back in. "Save your bullets."

"I can get them," she promised.

"You don't even know if you're hitting anything back there. You should save the few bullets we've got left."

"I've got to try," she insisted.

She leaned out the window again but another bullet hit the toolbox in the back with a metallic crunch. Deanna squealed and popped back inside. Sean imagined the metal buckling around the hole the bullet left behind and thanked God it hadn't gone all the way through the truck and into his spine.

"Better if you just stay down."

This time she didn't argue. She cowered, hugging her knees. She was so tough, but he could still see the fear she was trying to hide.

A picture of her barrel-racing popped in his head. He saw her bolting across the start line at top speed, leaning across her horse's wide back with her legs out, her blond hair streaming behind her, her eyes fixed on the prize. Fearless. That was Deanna Jackson.

He quickly squeezed her knee. "It's going to be okay," he promised. "We've come this far. It's not going to end here."

He glared into the rearview mirror. He'd brought her here. It was his responsibility to make sure he fulfilled that promise.

The tires hit loose gravel, sending the Ford's back end into a fishtail slide. Sean countersteered, struggling to regain traction and to right the truck. If they could only get to the paved road ahead, they'd have a smoother ride. But the pavement would also make it easier for Rex's brand-new rig to catch up. Rex would beat them in a speed race every time. At least this bumpy road leveled the playing field a bit.

Sean leaned across the bench seat, keeping

his left hand on the steering wheel and his head up only high enough to see where they were headed. No use keeping it up there where it could get popped like the mirror and the toolbox.

When the tires hit the paved road, the difference was apparent immediately. There wasn't any more bumping or jostling. It was too quiet, eerie even, as they waited for the next gunshot.

This highway would lead them to town, but the descent was steep and there were no guardrails. He was driving way too fast for the curves, and there were worse ones coming up. One in particular made him really nervous. He would need both hands on the wheel to navigate them. He tried to sit up, but as soon as he lifted his head, another bullet connected with the back window.

The glass exploded with a sound like illegal firecrackers. Deanna screamed and ducked to avoid the flying shrapnel-like debris. Sean shoved her head even lower. "Keep down," he commanded.

Hot wind whistled through the shattered back window. It wasn't as if the glass had been some great barrier of protection for them, but it had felt like it. Now they had nothing between them and those bullets but air. Sean tried to assess the damage to Deanna while still keeping his eyes on the road. A streak of bright red blood rolled down her cheek. It looked like a minor wound, probably a cut from flying glass, but his vision turned the same blood red. His pulse thundered. How dare they hurt her like this!

"You okay?"

She nodded and looked up at him, her eyes wide.

With his eyes on her instead of the road, the truck wandered too close to the steep edge. His back tires spun on the shoulder's loose gravel, giving Sean a close-up view of the direction he did not want to go. Small stones tumbled down the steep ravine, bouncing and skipping out of sight.

"Stay on the road," Deanna pleaded.

Sean righted the truck, turning sharply into the next turn. Rex pulled back a bit, slowing to avoid a collision with the fishtailing Ford's back end. Sean decelerated, also.

"Why are you slowing down?"

"I can't maintain this speed around these curves. There's a ninety-degree turn up ahead."

It did feel wrong to slow down, but he had to do it. He didn't know how many times he'd driven this road in his lifetime. He knew every inch of it, and his gut told him they were going too fast. "There's no other way—I have to slow down."

Rex didn't waste any time covering the

distance between the two vehicles. Deanna glanced backward, doubt written all over her face. "I hope you know what you're doing."

The turn Sean was worried about was next, hidden from view until you were right on it. If a turn ever deserved to be described as *sharp* or *hairpin*, this one was it. As they approached it, Sean hit the brakes even more. Instantly he knew things were about to get ugly. Rex wasn't slowing down at all. The scene through the rearview mirror was like a reverse game of chicken playing out in slow motion.

It was human nature to avoid a collision at all costs, and that's what Rex chose to do. He swerved away from the obstacle before him.

It was a deadly mistake.

Everything around Sean slowed, like he'd stepped outside time. As Rex's truck took flight over the cliff edge, Sean was an observer instead of a participant. He wasn't hearing or thinking, maybe not even breathing. Then just as suddenly, his blood rushed to his brain, and he woke up. He pulled the truck over to the shoulder and jumped out of the cab, already in a sprint, Deanna at his heels.

They didn't speak as they looked down at the red pickup tumbling end over end down the ravine. Deanna covered her face. Sean reached for her, drawing her against his chest. And then the truck reached the bottom and burst into flames.

Deanna stepped back, numb. Sean had let her go too soon, and she missed the comfort of being wrapped in his strong arms. She wanted to keep her face buried in his chest, to avoid turning around and seeing the death below her for a while longer. But Sean had already clambered over the road's edge and was inching his way down the steep ravine, rocks skidding out from under his cowboy boots, before she finally snapped out of her daze and realized where he was going. She imagined him tumbling end over end like the truck had done, breaking his neck in the process.

"What are you doing?" she'd screamed down at him.

"I've got to get to them. Someone might have survived."

"Five minutes ago they were shooting at us and now you want to rescue them?" *Unbelievable!* "It'll take you forever to reach the bottom going that way."

He didn't slow down. Did he need her to spell it out for him? "Sean, stop! It's too late. Look at that smoke," she hollered at him. "No one is coming out of that truck alive. It's not your fault. It was an accident, and we've got to let someone know what happened. This could blow up fast with all that bitterbrush to burn."

And that's what finally changed his mind. She rolled her eyes as he climbed back up the hill. Of course it would be the appeal to the greater good that got through to him. He was just so...*good*. Too good for his own good. It was one of the reasons she'd never let herself entertain feelings for Sean in the past. She couldn't deny a renewed attraction to him, but she had to stop herself from acting on those feelings. No matter what she felt, Sean was too good for her. She thought only about herself.

The violence of the truck crash might've horrified her, but playing hero and trying to rescue those men hadn't even crossed her mind. She'd been aware only of feeling safe again. That awful chase was over, and there would be no more bullets. But Sean? He wanted to save his enemies.

They jogged back to the truck.

"Where to now?" she asked, buckling her seat belt.

"Town. We've got to tell someone that we just started the sixth fire."

SEVEN

Deanna fixed her gaze on the road's center yellow line, the old truck's vibration lulling her into a strange sense of quiet. Or was it shock?

Her stomach growled. When had she eaten last? The orange of the smoky sky outside the passenger-side window had deepened to neon tangerine. It must be getting close to dinnertime, but she didn't wear a watch, so she didn't know the exact time.

The adrenaline that had sustained her all afternoon was gone. Exhaustion pulled at her eyelids. If she leaned her head back, she'd give in to sleep, but what kind of nightmares might follow if she did? She allowed her eyelashes to rest against her cheeks briefly, but images of Rex Turner's somersaulting pickup truck made them flutter back open.

So many questions and theories bounced inside her brain. She should talk to Sean about them, but she couldn't organize her thoughts into individual words, let alone a conversation. Besides, shouting above the wind coming through the shot-out window behind them felt like too much effort.

It was Sean who finally broke the silence. "I don't think we've met the man behind this yet."

Deanna shifted away from a sharp piece of ripped upholstery that was poking her in the back and then turned to face Sean. "You don't think Rex Turner was in charge?"

"No."

"What about Greg Martin?"

He shook his head. "Not him, either."

"Explain," she said.

"They all acted scared, like they were trying to clean up a mess before they were blamed for letting it happen. There's always a hierarchy in these kind of things, and I don't think any of those men were the boss."

Sean listed off all the men they could identify. "Do any of them fit the profile of a leader?"

Deanna slumped back against the seat. Admitting she agreed with him meant accepting that they still weren't safe. Who knew when they'd ever be safe again? His theory did match her own impressions, though. She replayed the events of the past few hours, and she could come to only one conclusion: Sean was right.

"We can tick Rex Turner and Nathan Reid

off the list of suspects," she said. She didn't elaborate further, trying to keep her voice matter-of-fact. Their deaths had been so horrible. She didn't even want to think about that yet, let alone talk about it. She was thankful Sean moved on quickly.

"And Greg Martin has always been the sidekick type. I can't see him calling the shots on something like this," he said.

"So if not them, then who?"

"Nathan Reid talked about that Pritchard guy as if he was in charge. Maybe it's him, whoever he is. I don't know. But we have to find out who is calling the shots." Sean sighed heavily and leaned his head against the window next to him. "Until we know exactly who it is we are dealing with, we won't be safe."

As he spoke his concerns, a new thought dawned in Deanna's mind. It unfolded slowly, giving her time to adjust to its enormity. If it had taken shape any faster, the weight of the fear the thought brought with it might have crushed her. They wouldn't be safe. And the people they loved weren't safe now, either.

Gram.

Greg Martin knew them too well. He was familiar with her family and Sean's, too. He would know what would hurt her the most. Deanna sat up straight, the blood draining from her face. She felt ill. "You have to take me to Gram."

"I told you I would," he said. "After the sheriff."

She shook her head. "No, I changed my mind. That'll take too long."

"But we agreed. After we report the fire, we can go home."

She should have thought of Gram sooner. Gram would have put her first, no matter what. She always did.

Sean pleaded his case. "We have to get help, if not for those men, then at least to stop the spread of more fire."

And then he said the worst thing possible. "It's the right thing to do."

Her cheeks burned. Sean thought she didn't care as much as he did, but that wasn't true at all. She cared too much, more than she wanted to let herself feel, but who was he to dictate her conscience? To tell her what was right or wrong? It reminded her of Blake Ransford. He was always doing that to her, too.

"I understand that people just died back there. It's horrible, and I don't want to see that fire spread any more than you do. But *Gram*." Deanna squeezed the seat's edge and closed her eyes. Just saying Gram's name aloud made her sick with worry. "Sean, Gram is my whole world."

A choice dangled before her. Maybe her father was onto something with his flying-solo philosophy. It might be a lonely life, but at least he got to call the shots. That's all Deanna wanted. To have a little control for once, and nothing said she *had* to stay with Sean. She hadn't considered separating from him—at least not until they'd seen this thing through—but now that they faced an impasse, it was probably time to leave him so she could take care of her own issues.

"You're quiet," Sean said. "What are you thinking about?"

"Drop me off on your way," she said. "I'll walk to The Hangar."

Sean flinched as if she'd slapped him. "I'm taking the last exit off the highway to go to the courthouse. Taking you downtown first would add too much time, and we need to stick together."

"Why do we have to stick together?" she demanded. It sounded cold, but she had to be tough for Gram. That mattered far more than Sean's feelings right now. Besides, they were getting too cozy anyway. She would only end up hurting him in the long run. This was for the best.

He rubbed his eyes, battling with some internal debate. Finally, he spoke. "I'll do whatever you want. I still believe we need to get help first, but if it means splitting up, I'll go downtown first."

Gripping the steering wheel, he looked up at the truck's roof. Then he turned to her. His voice was gruff, almost a whisper, but she could still hear it above the wind when he asked, "Please, Deanna?"

Her heart lurched at how much feeling was behind his request. Another reason to make a clean break now rather than later.

Sean continued, "You wouldn't be in danger if I hadn't gotten you into this mess. Let me make sure you're safe before you go off on your own."

They wouldn't be in this danger if Sean hadn't hired her.

They wouldn't be in this danger if she hadn't insisted on landing in the meadow.

They could play the blame game all day long, but truth stared her in the face: the actual threat of spreading fire took priority over the perceived threat to Gram. That ravine was full of flash fuel and Deanna's conscience spoke for itself. With no cell service, they had a duty to deliver the news in person. Taking her to The Hangar first really would add too much time. If she insisted they do this her way and then the fire spread, all the blame would land on her and her selfishness.

"Okay. We'll go for help first," she acquiesced and then turned to stare at Sean, determined to deliver her next message loud and clear. "But Gram better be okay."

He nodded slowly. "She will be."

Sean parked next to the courthouse annex and turned to Deanna. "Hopefully, this won't take too long."

"It better not."

He read her rigid body language. She wasn't giving him an inch. Anything that went wrong would be his fault, and keeping her with him wasn't going to be easy, either. She could change her mind and bolt at any minute.

"We'll be in and out, I promise. Report what we know, then we're out of there. Maybe they can send someone to check on your grandma while we fill out reports," he said.

The laser-sharp look she shot him was impressive. "I don't want them to send someone. I want to see she's safe with my own eyes."

It was fear that was making her mean. He understood it. Sean worried about his family, too, but it was different for him. Uncle Paul could fend for himself, and his mother and grandmother had moved to Spokane a few years ago after his grandfather passed away. His loved ones were almost a three-hour drive away from this danger. He understood Deanna's urgency. Arlene Jackson was right here, and she was alone with no way for them to warn her.

He tried to put a hand on her shoulder, but Deanna flinched away from it. He let his hand drop back to his lap, his face flushing. What had he thought would happen? That after their harrowing afternoon together, she would somehow suddenly be swept off her feet?

Without looking at her, he said, "Making sure your Gram is safe is our next step, I promise."

"Let's stop talking about it, then, and get this over with," she said.

He was so terrible with women. What should he have said to her? Even if he'd had all the right words, it wouldn't have mattered anyway. Deanna wanted only one thing right now. The best thing he could do for her would be to get in and out of the sheriff's office as quickly as possible.

Walking through the parking lot, they passed a hodgepodge of the department's fleet of vehicles—a few Ford sedans, a couple of Suburban SUVs, a diesel pickup—all of them displaying the same sheriff's department logo. Deanna stopped and stared at the final car in the lineup.

She flipped her arm out, catching Sean across the gut. "That's it."

"Huh?" Now what?

She kept her arm against him and pointed with her other hand at a forest green Jeep Cherokee. "That's the car I saw by the shed in the meadow."

Disbelief froze Sean in place as he stared at the Jeep. Had someone from the sheriff's department really been up there? Everything had happened so fast it was possible that Deanna was mistaken. Jeeps were common enough. Sean hoped that was the case because the alternative was too scary. Sheriff Johnson was his best friend. Sean had always known Jim to be a man of integrity and moral conviction. If his department was somehow compromised, or—Sean shuddered at his next thought—if Jim wasn't the man Sean thought him to be, then there was no one else left to help them. He needed Deanna to be wrong.

EIGHT

Deanna was familiar with the older, prettier courthouse next door, but what reason would she have ever had to come into this annex and see the sheriff? She glanced around the fluorescent-lit room. Could they trust whoever was in here? It was doubtful that Sean believed her about the Jeep. He was too much of a Sheriff Johnson fan. He'd never believe this department could be anything but on the up and up if it meant implicating his best friend.

"Can I help you?" a female voice asked from behind a bank of dispatch equipment.

"Um, yes. We need to report—" Deanna began.

"Sean!"

The plump, ginger-haired woman hustled around the desk, brushing past Deanna in her haste to wrap Sean up in a warm embrace. Deanna closed her mouth, not bothering to finish the sentence she'd started.

The woman held Sean at arm's length, appraising him. "Oh my goodness, sweetie, what happened? You look beat up."

Sean gave her a warm smile and said, "You should see the other guy."

"I can imagine," she said, embracing him a second time.

Deanna stepped away from them and tucked her thumbs into her back pockets. She looked up at the ceiling to avoid watching them. Was she jealous? She didn't have any claim on Sean, and it wasn't like this matronly woman would be any kind of rival even if she did. But the obvious loving connection between the two of them left her hollow. This other woman was in her spot. Sean's arms around her at the crash site had been warm and comforting. He'd protected her from watching Rex's truck plunging to the bottom of the ravine. Deanna wanted back in those arms, where she could pretend that this day had never happened. Where she could feel safe again.

Deanna clenched her teeth, disgusted with herself. She was just shaken up and missing Gram, that's all. She shouldn't be jealous; she should be annoyed. This was Sean's idea of "in and out"? This woman looked like she was winding up for a long-winded walk down memory lane, and they didn't have time for that.

"Good to see you, Sue," Sean said. "We need to report an accident and possibly a new fire."

"You mean that crash site out on Tunk Road? That was reported a bit ago. Already sent men out there."

Deanna's nostrils flared and she glared at Sean. They could have skipped this stop altogether.

"I hope they get that fire put out before it gets close to your place," the dispatcher said.

"Me, too," Sean said.

That thought hadn't occurred to Deanna. Sean's ranch was already threatened from the east. The last thing he needed was to worry about new flames coming from the west. That ravine had been a tinderbox. It could easily blow up the hill. It was more evidence of how selfish she was. She had been so focused on what coming here first was costing her. She'd never bothered to consider what it was costing Sean.

He put a hand on the small of Deanna's back, pulling her into the conversation. A thrill traveled through her at the touch and at the thoughtfulness it represented.

They'd never be a good match. Sean was too laid-back to put up with a hothead like her. She'd end up walking all over him, and he'd end up resenting her for it. But when Sean did find the right girl, whoever she was, that woman would be treated like a queen. Deanna couldn't help but admit to herself that she *was* jealous of that girl.

"Deanna, this is Sue Lloyd. Sue's a friend from church," Sean said. "We're in a home group together."

Deanna stuck her hand out to shake, but instead of gripping her hand in return, Sue folded her up into a voluminous hug. Deanna awkwardly patted the woman a few times on her back. As a rule, she did not hug strangers. She met Sean's eyes, begging him to take charge and hurry things along.

Sue held Deanna out at arm's length. Her turn for inspection. "Oh, honey, you look a little worse for the wear yourself." Sue's forehead creased. "Are you guys okay?"

A lump formed in Deanna's throat. The concern in Sue's voice was too much for her to handle. They'd reported the fire. Could they go now?

"We're actually hoping to see Jim," Sean told Sue. "Is he in? It's important."

Before Sue could answer, a honeyed voice from behind them spoke. "Sean Loomis and Deanna Jackson. Looks like we've got ourselves a little high school reunion going on here."

Deanna rolled her eyes. She'd know that

lazy drawl anywhere. Sure enough, when she turned, she found Austin Mills, a guy she'd dated in high school, leaning against the doorjamb.

Austin was dressed for the part of deputy, but the official uniform looked more like a costume on him. Deanna almost laughed out loud. Austin a deputy? She'd never be able to take him seriously.

Sean mumbled a halfhearted greeting. "Austin."

There had never been much love lost between the two men. They were polar opposites. But between Deanna and Austin—that was a different story. There had been plenty of love lost there. Dating him had been a huge mistake.

Sue frowned. The look she gave Austin told Deanna that she wasn't much of a fan, either.

Without acknowledging Austin, Sue said, "Sorry, Sean. Sheriff's not in the office much these days. But he'll be at the high school gym at seven tonight for a town meeting. There's going to be a press conference about the fires."

She glanced at her watch. "You've got about an hour and a half or so."

Good. Now they could get out of there and get to Gram. They'd done their duty. Time to go.

Still leaning in the doorway, Austin crossed

his arms and flashed his "my daddy bought me expensive braces" smile, never breaking eye contact with Deanna.

"In the meantime, looks like you're stuck with me," he said. "What can I do for you, Dee?"

Deanna glared at Austin. In her mind, she pronounced his name like she was spitting out sour food. "I think we'll come back later…"

Sean maneuvered Deanna toward the door. "We'll come back when Jim's here. Deanna's got to get to The Hangar and check on her grandmother anyway."

Austin stood to full height. "What's wrong with Arlene?"

"Nothing. I hope. We just had a crazy…" Deanna looked to Sean to finish the sentence. How could she explain everything they'd been through?

Sean hesitated. "It's a long story."

"They were up at the Tunk crash site," Sue said.

"Whatever you have to do, it can wait." Austin gestured with a nod of his head. "Come on back."

He led them down a hallway to a conference room. He waited for them to sit and then said, "So tell me this story."

Sean and Deanna made eye contact. Where

did they even begin? They both spoke, talking over each other. Deanna waved at Sean. "You start."

Sean's mouth quirked to the side, his brows furrowing. Deanna could imagine his brain sifting through the afternoon's events, trying to figure out the relevant details. She was doing the same thing. "I had a valuable horse go missing, and Deanna took me up in her plane to look for him."

"So you want to report a missing animal? You'll need to contact the state brand inspector," Austin droned, already bored.

"No. That's not it," Sean said, clearly frustrated. "It's what we found while we were looking that we need to talk to you about."

"We found a hidden landing strip," Deanna added.

They attempted to piece together the crazy story. They told Austin about the drugs and the guns, about Sean being knocked out and the two of them tied up. They told him about their narrow escape and the unorthodox landing in Sean's alfalfa field. They finished with Rex Turner's crash and their concern for Gram's safety.

Austin's chair squeaked as he lounged back in it, raising his long quarterback arms behind his head. His styled sandy curls and his too-perfect, symmetrical face made Austin look like he belonged in a Hollywood soap opera instead of sitting here in a small-town sheriff's department.

"Wow. Rough day," he said.

The dry tinder of Deanna's temper sparked. She popped up from her chair. "Yeah. Rough. Did you even bother to write any of that down, *Deputy* Mills?"

Sean's hand covered hers. He could try to calm her down all he wanted, but it wouldn't work. She wouldn't let Austin demean them like this.

"I don't need to write it down." Austin smirked and tapped his temple. "Like a steel trap."

He leaned forward on his forearms. "Look, I understand. You've been through a lot today. You've got a right to be freaked out, but I'm not getting all worked up about it, because you didn't tell me anything I didn't already know. It's already been taken care of."

"How?" Sean asked, leaning forward to mirror Austin's posture, his eyes set in a steely stare. Something flashed between the two men that Deanna couldn't decipher. As Sean sat up to his full height, they looked like two bucks about to lock horns.

Austin continued, "You can rest easy tonight because we've already made arrests."

Arrests? Deanna sat back down, relaxing a bit. So that Jeep up in the hills had been one of the good guys? She was grateful that she'd misjudged the situation. Maybe this nightmare was about to be over after all. Maybe there was no threat to Gram. It was over.

"Who?" Sean asked. He didn't sound as relieved.

Austin stood. "Can't discuss an ongoing case with you, Sean, but I will assure you that the two of you are safe now. This smuggling operation has been cut off at the knees. After the DEA gets involved, they'll all be too busy defending themselves to worry about you two."

He slapped paper and pens in front of them and said, "I'll just need your statements, and as soon as things calm down with the fires, I'm sure Sheriff Johnson or a detective will be in touch."

"That's it?" Sean said.

"That's it." Austin walked toward the door. Before he left the room, he turned and said, "Frankly, Loomis, I'm glad to hear you weren't involved with all that illegal activity on your land. You're fortunate to have a friend like

Sheriff Johnson to defend you. He kept insisting that you were one of the good guys."

Austin's face looked doubtful.

It was Sean's turn to stand. "Don't give me that, Mills. I'm the same guy I've always been, and you know it."

Austin's mouth moved up in a slow smirk. "Been a while, Sean. People change. Most aren't the same person they were in high school."

"Well, I am," Sean insisted.

"Good to know," Austin answered. He made eye contact with Deanna and winked. "Wait here. I'll be back." Then he walked from the room.

Fuming, Deanna grabbed a black ink pen and started scribbling her side of the story. She needed to get it all out and her blood pressure down. Who did he think he was treating them like this? Using that infuriating, condescending tone? And then he thought he could wink at her like the good ole days? He had another thing coming if he thought that. Austin Mills had used up all his charm in high school. Sean might not have changed since then, but Deanna certainly had.

Her handwriting was loopy and passionate, her story filling up both the front and back of the page. When she reached the end, she slammed the last period into place and tossed the pen and paper away from her as if they burned her hand.

"There." She crossed her arms.

"What's wrong, Deanna?" Sean asked, his voice calm. He set his pen down, finished. His tiny, neat writing only covered the front of the paper. How had he kept the story so short?

"Austin," Deanna huffed. "I can't stand him."

Sean chuckled. "You used to like him just fine."

"Well, not anymore. Unlike you, I am not the same person I was in high school."

"Yes, you are."

How could he say that? "No, I am not!"

"Yes," Sean insisted, his dark eyes locking on hers across the table. "You are."

Her voice rose in volume, shrill to her own ears. "Do you really think I could be interested in a guy like Austin Mills now?"

"No," Sean agreed, grinning. "At least, I hope not."

He tapped the paper in front of him with the pen. She could see he was weighing his words carefully, something she never did. Thinking before speaking her mind? Not her strong suit.

"Okay. So your preference in men might have changed—we can both agree that's a good thing—and you might have matured since then." He paused. The pen tapped harder, bouncing out of his reach. Deanna leaned forward, shocked by just how much she wanted to hear what he would say. To know how he saw her.

Sean retrieved the pen and held on to it with both hands. "Who you are at the core is exactly the same girl you've always been," he said, his intense, dark gaze connecting with hers. "Smart, tough, talented."

His smile lines crinkled around the corners of his eyes as he added, "Too good for a bum like Mills."

His words stunned her. She didn't want to blink and break the eye contact. She wanted to search his eyes for more. All the compliments she had ever heard from men in the past had always been about her appearance, but Sean had just said that he saw a smart woman, a woman with depth and value. She wasn't that woman but she wanted to be. Realizing how much she cared about his opinion of her surprised and scared her. So she moved on.

"What are we going to do now?" she asked. "Forget about all that happened today? Move on like Austin wants us to do?"

Sean pursed his lips and slowly shook his

head. "Of course not. I don't trust Austin Mills as far as I can toss him. Let's get out of here before he stops us and go pick up your grandmother."

"And then what?" she asked.

"Then we find the sheriff and get some real answers."

NINE

The rusty old pickup slipped into the first empty space on Main Street. Deanna was impressed with how easily Sean parallel-parked the Beast, but she didn't waste any words complimenting him. Gram's safety was the only thing either one of them should be wasting energy on.

"She better be okay," she said. If she kept repeating it with enough authority, maybe she could make it true.

"She will be," Sean said once again, but Deanna recognized the forced confidence in his voice. More wishful thinking.

He hadn't cut the engine before she wrenched open her door and hopped out onto the sidewalk. She ran for The Hangar, remembering the angry men who'd chased them through the meadow. She heard again the obscenities and murderous threats they'd hurled at them in between their gunshots. Gram was her only family, the only security she'd ever known. Greg Martin would know that Gram was the surest way to control her. Austin said the men up there were all in jail already, though. That she and Sean were safe and didn't have anything to worry about. But what if they hadn't really gotten them all? Or what if some of those men had gotten here before the sheriff made his arrests? The thought of those men touching Gram infuriated her.

Deanna pushed herself faster. Her throat was so tight she could hardly swallow down the anxiety. She couldn't wait to see Gram, to hug her, to catch the scent of Gram's hand cream as her soft hand patted Deanna's cheek.

Gram would be inside. She'd laugh at Deanna for being so paranoid.

Deanna stopped several paces back from the door. The fancy chalkboard sign that read Come In We're OPEN had been flipped over. It now read Sorry We're CLOSED, Please Come Again. Fear wrapped its fingers around Deanna's throat and squeezed.

It was too early to be closed.

She yanked hard but the lock held fast. Pounding on the glass with her open palm, she called, "Gram. It's me. Open up."

There was no answer. Deanna cupped her hands and peered inside. She couldn't see anyone in there, but her eyes settled on a small lump of soft leather on the floor against the far wall.

She pressed her forehead against the glass. It was her purse. She remembered dropping it there this morning when she opened. There wasn't anything of value in it except…

"My keys," she moaned.

She'd been so nervous about defying Blake when they left she'd grabbed her Cessna key off its hook on the office wall and forgot to grab her purse. Dumb.

Deanna straightened. She grabbed her right elbow with her left hand and pulled it into herself to think. She bit down on her thumbnail. Should she break the glass? It was totally possible that Gram had grown tired of waiting for her and had simply closed up early. But she couldn't shake the sense of foreboding. This didn't feel right to her at all.

If only she had the phone in her purse and working cell service. Then she could call Gram and ask her. Man, she'd taken instant communication for granted. She never would again.

Sean stood still beside her, his expression stoic and unreadable. What would he do?

The answer was immediate. Sean would pray. It was what Gram would do, too.

A flood of memories hit Deanna. She was

in her childhood bedroom, surrounded by her stuffed animals and her toy horses. Back then, Jesus had felt close. He wasn't just Gram's God; He was hers, too. She'd never missed Him as much as she did right now.

She knew exactly the moment when her faith began to dry up. Dad had been between jobs and home visiting her and Gram. He walked in on one of Deanna's tea parties, and she introduced all of her guests to him.

"This is Carrie Ann and this is Rosy," she said, holding up each doll to make the introduction. Then she held up one of her model horses. "And this is Thunder—he's a Tennessee walking horse. And oh yeah, you can't see Him, but Jesus is sitting right there."

Dad's face turned the color of one of Gram's tomatoes. "Who's sitting there, Dee-girl?"

"That's Jesus," she said, smiling.

"Mom!" he yelled toward the kitchen. "What kind of garbage are you feeding Deanna?"

Tears flooded her eyes. Deanna didn't know what she'd done that was so wrong. His anger scared her. When he saw her watery eyes, he ruffled her hair and said, "Deanna, baby, God is a fairy tale used to control weak-minded people. We aren't weak people. We take care of ourselves."

And she'd believed him. That was all it took.

No more praying or having tea parties with Jesus. She would have done anything to make her daddy love her enough to stay. A week later he was gone again.

Deanna looked at the mocking closed sign staring her in the face. Sean and Gram weren't weak. They were stronger than Dad ever was. And Gram was far too precious to leave any base uncovered. What could it hurt?

Jesus...

It had been so long it felt like priming the old rusty pump she used to fill her horse's water trough.

Help me find Gram.

Make her be okay.

There was so much more she should say but that was the best she could come up with for now. She tacked on a *please* and *amen* for good measure. That's what you were supposed to do, right?

She faced Sean, searching his face for reassurance, looking to him to confirm that her first prayer in years would be rewarded. How long would it take for God to answer?

Movement drew her gaze down to his hands. He twiddled his fingers, tapping them on his pant leg as if he were playing the piano. They never stopped their constant nervous motion. She jerked her gaze back up to his face. His right eye twitched, betraying him. Sean was worried about Gram. He was afraid something had happened to her. It was probably already too late.

Red rage colored her vision as she balled her fists. "I told you we needed to come here first! But you wouldn't listen. You always have to do the right thing. And then it didn't even matter. Someone else had already reported the crash and the fire before us. We wasted all that time!"

"Check the back door."

Deanna sprinted toward the alley. As she turned the corner, she heard Sean's footsteps echoing off the brick buildings behind her. She was mad at him, but she was glad he was there. She didn't want to face this alone.

The alleyway spread the full length of Main Street. It was the ugly side, the part that customers never saw. The only thing that distinguished each business from the other was the black stenciled name spray-painted on each white door.

Deanna slowed when she reached her blue Mazda still parked where she'd left it earlier that morning. She sighed at the sight of something normal. That had to be a good sign.

But as she passed the car, she came to such an abrupt stop Sean had to skid on the gravel to keep from colliding into her back.

"What?" he asked her.

Her world spun. Deanna pointed.

The Hangar's back door was wide open. It hung awkwardly on broken hinges.

She gulped and then stated the obvious. "It's open."

Sean pulled Deanna back, preventing her from running through the open door.

"I'll go in," he said.

"If you think I'm waiting out here like a good little girl, you've got something else coming." She squirmed and thrashed, making it almost impossible to hold on to her.

"Let go of me," she spit out between gritted teeth.

"Slow down," he begged.

"If you say one word about a making a plan first…"

"I'm not letting you run in there half-cocked like some crazy woman. Let me figure out—"

"Enough! I told you to stop thinking so much and to start acting. Let me in there to find Gram."

He held up his hands in surrender. "You said yourself that this is my fault. How would both of us going in there and getting our heads shot off help your grandmother? All I'm asking is that you let me check it out first."

She pressed her lips into a thin line, considering it.

He tried a new approach. "At least let me lead the way?"

She didn't like it, but she'd stopped arguing. He took that as a green light and stepped around her, scanning the area for signs of trouble. The only thing suspicious so far was the open door.

"Do you still have your pistol?" he asked her.

"So now you can handle a gun better than me, too?"

He thought better of reminding her of her failure to use it in the meadow and gestured for her to hand over the pistol. "Come on, Dee. Don't make me go in there unarmed."

She pulled the gun out of her waistband. Placing it into his outstretched hand, Deanna wrapped her own fingers around his for a moment, her touch light and tender. She bit her lip before she said, "Be careful."

His shoulders slumped as relief washed over him. If she cared about his safety, maybe she didn't hate him too much. "Does this mean you forgive me?"

"Find my grandmother, and I'll consider it." She dropped his hands and freed him to go. Sean stepped toward the broken door.

"Sean?" she whispered.

He turned. "I'm afraid of what we're going to find in there," she said.

"Me, too," he admitted.

She hugged her arms around her waist. "Okay. No more talking. Let's find Gram."

Sean aimed the handgun at the door and pressed against it, opening it enough to step through. He entered the hallway, gun raised. His breaths came out in shallow gulps. He wasn't a cop, but his instinct told him the gun should lead the way and not his head.

"Arlene? Are you in here?" he called.

He crept along the hallway, keeping his right shoulder against the wall, and Deanna mimicked his moves. He stepped one boot over the other until he reached the first door. He gently kicked it open, revealing the small bathroom.

Nothing.

He let out the breath he was holding. One room down.

The storage room was next. He flipped on the light and stepped inside. Espresso beans and broken syrup bottles littered the floor. Supplies were strewn everywhere, shelves cleaned off as if someone had taken an arm along them and swiped everything off them onto the ground and then dumped the shelving units on top of it all for added effect.

Deanna gasped and stumbled against the doorjamb for support.

Sean crunched across broken glass, kicking paper cups and plastic lids out of his way as he went. His boots felt heavier than usual as they pulled against the sticky mess. He wondered if the mess had come from a struggle. Had Arlene tried to fight them off in here? He wasn't sure. It felt more like a message to Deanna. A warning to keep her mouth shut.

He quickly cleared the rest of the back. The click of the light in each room revealed more damage, while each of Deanna's gasps broke his heart a little more.

The front customer area had been spared. The men had probably avoided this area, worried about being seen or heard through the picture windows. Sean breathed a prayer of gratitude that this part of The Hangar had been untouched. Everywhere he looked, he saw evidence of Deanna's personality and hard work.

His eyes roamed the room, taking in the details. Her love for flying was everywhere. Framed vintage aviation posters lined the warm golden walls, and in the far corner a polished World War I–era propeller leaned against the wall. There was a perfect balance between masculine wood and leather and feminine touches. It was a room that invited you to stay. It had

Deanna's touch, and Sean didn't think he would have been able to stand seeing it destroyed, too. Not after all she'd endured today.

He glanced at the clock on the wall. It was nearing seven o'clock, still almost an hour and a half before the sun would set. These men had been so bold, attacking Deanna's business while it was still light enough outside to get caught. He felt a quiver of relief travel up his back, thankful they hadn't been able to deliver their message to Deanna in person. What would they have done to her if they'd found her here?

He swallowed as he thought of Arlene in here alone with no one to protect her. She was made of the same sturdy stock as Deanna, but she wasn't tough enough to take on a gang of men all by herself.

He rubbed his temples, replaying the afternoon's events all over again. Guilt threatened to pull him to the ground, more powerful than gravity. He should have listened to Deanna and come here first. It wasn't like seeing Austin Mills had made the situation better for anyone.

"Arlene?" he called once more, mostly because he didn't know what else to do yet, not because he really thought she was in the building.

Deanna's voice echoed through the darkness. "You know she's not here."

He closed his eyes and prayed that God would show him how to help Deanna. He prayed for Arlene's safety.

When he opened his eyes, Deanna was standing in the room. She stroked the polished wood of the propeller in the corner.

"My dad gave it to me when I opened," she said in a monotone voice. "He said he was proud of me. It was the only time he'd ever said it."

Sean reached for her but she shook her head, warning him not to touch her. He prayed again, this time asking God to show him how in the world he was going to convince Deanna to forgive him.

TEN

Tears stung like tiny acupuncture needles behind Deanna's eyes. Sean's peace in the middle of her storm felt like a slap in the face, as if he'd betrayed her somehow. Her livelihood was scattered around his feet in shambles and what was he doing? Standing there with his eyes closed again. Praying.

Disgusted, she turned to walk back outside, but she stopped at the storage room. She covered her nose and mouth, the cloying smell threatening to suffocate her. She turned in circles trying to take in all of the damage. The smell of the various syrups she used to make the custom drinks on The Hangar's menu typically comforted her, but the fumes they emitted from being dumped together in these massive quantities gagged her now. Odd flavor combinations like English toffee with peppermint, strawberry and Irish cream, clashed and assaulted her senses.

The desperation was as heavy as if all of the shelves full of supplies had fallen on top of her, crushing her. Tears welled, but if she let them fall, she'd drown. She'd end up curled on the floor in a fetal position, indulging her pain instead of finding Gram. She didn't need to cry; she needed to *do* something.

She didn't have to turn around to know Sean was behind her and lashing out at him seemed like a good place to start. "Why do you even bother?"

"Bother with what?"

"Praying," she accused, the bitterness dripping from the word as if it were a wet sock. What was wrong with her? Why did she care what happened between him and his God? Asking for God's help wasn't a personal affront to her. Still, it felt like one.

"Seems like every time I catch you doing it, something worse happens." She flipped around to face him. "Why don't you do us all a favor and knock it off."

Sean didn't look shocked. He wasn't mad, either. His calm ticked her off all the more.

"You think God did this," he said gently. Was that a question or a statement?

Did she blame God? He probably just didn't care. "No, I don't think He did this. But it happened on His watch, didn't it?" Deanna wrapped her arms around herself, trying to warm the odd chill she felt. It was too hot to be this cold.

"I prayed for Gram," she admitted. "Out front. I asked for His help."

Sean remained silent, waiting for her to spill her guts.

"And where is she?" Deanna took a step toward him, wanting to get a rise out of him. Her finger stabbed at his shoulder. "Where is your horse, Sean? I'm sure you prayed about that, right?" He said nothing, and before she could regret it, she spit out her next spiteful question. "Where is your father?"

He winced. Eventually, he said, "Praying isn't like dropping a quarter in a vending machine and expecting a prize to pop out. Yeah, I wanted to have answers, but I don't get to tell God how it's done."

"Like I said," she huffed, "why bother, then?"

"Because I can't do it on my own," Sean said, sweeping out his hand, indicating the shambles of her life. "Can you, Deanna?"

"Whatever," she snarled and stomped away.

"Deanna," Sean called after her. She didn't face him, but she stopped to listen.

"You wouldn't want God to do your bidding," he said. "You wouldn't want Him to be that small."

She fled. Being mad at God felt too good to stick around and let Sean pacify her. She burst out into the alley, leaving behind the syrupy smell. But the smell outside was equally suffocating. She brushed away a fleck of ash from her nose. And then another one. She looked into the sky. The smoke was getting worse and ash was starting to fall like snowflakes. She sucked in a deep breath and instantly regretted it.

At first her throat tickled, but the sensation escalated to a coughing fit. Less and less air flowed to her lungs. She couldn't stop hacking. She couldn't breathe.

She felt the soft pressure of Sean's large hand on her back.

"Sean, I can't breathe," she wheezed. She swiped at her watering eyes. "I can't breathe," she repeated, hearing the panicked tone of her voice before another round of violent coughing began. Her body started to tremble as pain burned under her rib cage.

He rubbed slow circles between her shoulder blades. "You're okay, Deanna. You're going to be okay."

It took so long to stop coughing, but eventually, the pain eased and she could breathe normally again. The falling ash clung to Sean's black hair, making it salt-and-pepper as if he'd aged decades before her eyes. He looked so wise and so kind. Her heart ached from the concern etched on his face.

She stepped closer. If he reached for her again, she wouldn't turn him away; she'd let him hold her, let him make her feel safe again. When had she become so needy?

"I'm failing, Sean," she whispered. "Nothing is ever enough. It doesn't matter how hard I work at The Hangar, or how many rodeos I win, or how many customers hire me to fly them somewhere. The Hangar is losing money. My plane is sitting in your alfalfa field. I'm going to lose it all." She inhaled sharply, blinking hard. "I can't lose Gram. She's all I've got."

He pulled her close, and she buried her face in his chest. His big hands kept rubbing circles between her shoulder blades. In the distance church bells rang, snapping her back into good sense. She counted seven gongs. She pulled back and wiped at her eyes, humiliated. One minute she was yelling at him, the next she was falling apart.

"Seven o'clock," Sean said. "Maybe Arlene closed up early so she could go to Jim's meeting." He sounded like he was trying to convince himself. "Maybe she's sitting there in the gym waiting for you right now."

"You better hope she is," Deanna said, trying to rouse her anger again. She wanted to keep blaming Sean and to make him pay, but the anger had dissipated. How could anyone stay mad at Sean Loomis for long?

It wasn't him she needed to be angry at anyway.

"Get in," she said, pointing at her car. "It's my turn to drive."

Sean scrunched up his mouth and didn't move. "You didn't see your tires."

All four tires had been slashed. She wasn't surprised, actually. She should have expected it. And she knew more was coming. The worst part was admitting that, like it or not, she was still dependent on Sean. Weak and needy. The very things she'd fought against her whole life. Gram would tell her, "Grin and bear it, girl."

She sighed, resigned. "Looks like we take the Beast, then."

The high school gymnasium was standing-room only, packed to capacity. Sean and Deanna pushed through the throng, trying to position themselves where they could search for Arlene without drawing attention to themselves.

"It's as crowded in here as it was for the basketball championship last year," Sean said, pulling at the collar of his T-shirt. He liked wide-open spaces. Not crowds. This was too tight for his liking.

"Lot of the same people are here," Deanna whispered.

"A little different mood, though," he muttered. On the night of the championship, there had been none of this weighty anxiety that pressed people into their seats now.

The squeaky wooden bleachers overflowed with families, while ruddy-faced ranchers stood guard on each side of the stands, too full of pride and nervous energy to sit down.

"Any sign of her?" he asked.

"No," Deanna said, lifting wide, fear-filled eyes to him. She reminded him of the white-tail deer on his property. A startled deer could make it a quarter of a mile across a field before Sean could even blink. If he wasn't careful, he feared Deanna might take flight in the same way. He pushed away the urge to restrain her, to force her to stay right here where he could protect her. That would be the worst approach possible for Deanna. He was working with borrowed time. If he couldn't produce her grandmother soon, nothing would stop her from bolting.

The faces he searched were pinched and hungry for good news. They listened to Jim Johnson talking, but all they really wanted from their sheriff was reassurance, to be told that Kinakane would remain untouched by the angry flames marching toward it. Sean recognized most of the people there, but he couldn't see Arlene Jackson among them.

Grabbing Deanna's hand, he put his lips to her ear and whispered, "Don't leave." When she stiffened, he quickly added, "Please, Deanna." He might be a fool when it came to women, but he was smart enough to know that no one ordered Deanna Jackson to do anything.

Sean nodded toward Jim. "You're not going to be able to find her without his help. We need a plan."

"You and your plans," she hissed. "It's always 'wait a little bit longer' or 'after we talk with the sheriff.'"

She jerked her hand out of his. "You can't make a plan for everything. Sometimes you just have to act."

A rancher turned and glared at them. "You need to take it outside or shut up," he said. "I'm here to listen to Sheriff Johnson talk, not you two lovebirds bickering behind me."

Sean's cheeks burned; he felt like a teenager being shushed in church. Deanna's face flamed, too, but Sean wasn't sure if that was anger or embarrassment. "Sorry," he mumbled, hoping to defuse the situation before Deanna's temper flared.

Sean's fingers twitched at his sides. His pleas weren't working. He wanted Jim's help. There was no doubt they needed his professional perspective. Deanna was wrong—they did need a plan, but if he couldn't convince her of that, he'd have to leave with her.

Sean moved his body between Deanna and the door. He leaned in near her ear again, attempting one last time to talk sense to her. "She could still be here. You can't see everyone in this room."

Deanna huffed, but she turned back around. Sean exhaled. She wasn't leaving yet. It was a temporary victory, but he'd take it.

In front of the bleachers, metal folding chairs held reporters. A few camera crews were set up on the baseline, their cameras aimed at center court, where Jim stood behind a music stand that someone had turned into a makeshift podium.

"Come on, Sheriff," someone called out, interrupting the presentation. "Just spit it out. Is the fire coming or not?"

Under different circumstances, Sean would've been one of these ranchers. He'd be standing with his own arms crossed, braced to hear the worst. His only concern would be protecting his livelihood and his livestock, protecting the home that had been in both sides of his family for generations. The Callaghan side had come straight from Ireland several generations before him, and the Loomis family were natives. They'd always been here. Regardless of the day's events or how justified Sean was to be distracted, his home should still be his focus. The fire was coming whether he was paying attention or not. He had to know what was at stake. He tried his best to stop worrying about Deanna long enough to hear the sheriff's words.

"As of this evening," Jim said, "Kinakane has been upgraded to level-two evacuation notice."

Sean's stomach tightened. A ripple of anxious whispers scampered across the bleachers. The media people sat up, suddenly awake. Jim had just handed them a sound bite for the eleven-o'clock news. Reporters waved their hands in the air, trying to interrupt him, but Jim barreled through, ignoring them.

"The official level change means there is significant threat to this area and you all need to be ready to evacuate," he said. His sigh was audible through the PA system. He looked over the heads of the waving media and fixed his gaze on his friends and neighbors in the stands. Genuine concern and weariness oozed from him. Politics came with the job, but this sheriff cared more about his constituents' safety than he did about pandering to the media. Sean ached for his friend, sure he couldn't even fathom the load on Jim's shoulders, couldn't imagine all he'd dealt with in the past week.

Jim continued, "I've been all over the county. I've seen firsthand the devastation to people's homes and livestock. How there hasn't been any loss of human life yet..." He paused, collecting himself. "Well, I thank God for that."

Sean had seen the dead cows and the burned-out houses on the news, but Jim had actually been there. He'd helped sound the alarm to evacuate, had comforted those who had lost it all.

"I just got word that the Red Cross is packing up their temporary shelter," Jim said. "They've determined Kinakane isn't safe enough for the refugees. Bottom line is this, people—if you don't absolutely have to be here, now is the time to go."

The sheriff kept his eyes locked on the crowd, unblinking. "Conditions change fast. We're doing our best to keep the Facebook page current and local media outlets updated, but we can't predict everything. Don't wait for someone to knock on your door. Evacuate immediately if you're at all concerned."

Jim waited, letting the gravity of his words register. Leave it to Jim to give it to them bluntly. Sean could always count on Jim to tell it to him straight, and Sean couldn't wait to talk with him alone.

Deanna bounced on her toes, her eyes still scanning the crowd. Had she heard a single word? She might be in denial, but Sean didn't blame her. She didn't have room mentally or emotionally to worry about one more thing. And that was okay, because Sean was doing enough worrying for the both of them.

And then Deanna gasped. Her fingernails bit into Sean's skin.

"What is it?" he asked. She looked so pale.

"Farside of the bleachers," she whispered. "By the side door."

In the shadows, behind the bleachers where no one else was looking, stood Arlene Johnson. Sean's lips turned up at the corners, ready to form a smile, but before he could enjoy the relief, the moment shattered. His stomach plummeted. Behind Arlene stood their old classmate Greg Martin. Wasn't he one of the men Austin Mills had assured them would no longer be a threat?

Sean balled his fists. Greg was slowly guiding Arlene toward the far exit. He wanted to sprint across the gym to rescue her, but Sean was facing another whitetail deer situation. Move too fast, and he'd startle the other man and lose Arlene in the process.

Greg locked eyes with Sean and lifted his finger to his lips. Slowly, he moved his other hand out from behind Arlene's back to reveal a black pistol he held in it, sending Sean an abundantly clear warning.

ELEVEN

When Deanna was ten years old, she walked too close to an unbroken stallion who didn't want to load into a horse trailer. He'd kicked unexpectedly, connecting with her chest. The force sent her flying, slamming her against the barn wall. She slid to the ground, shocked from the pain and lack of air, unable to move. It really was a wonder it hadn't killed her.

This felt like that. She was rooted to the ground and helpless to do anything but stare. Greg and Gram seemed just as shocked to see her. Who would react first? Sean's biceps bulged under her hand. The seconds stretched.

Her brain grasped for a solution as her eyes frantically searched for help. She wanted to scream, to force everyone to notice the sinister drama playing out in the dark corner of the gym. But the crowd was too fixated on the sheriff, everyone completely oblivious to anything but their own concerns.

Fire, fire, fire. That's all anyone thought about anymore, all anyone could talk about. That threat was still miles away. How could they not sense the real danger happening right beside them?

Greg took another step back, pulling Gram along with him, so close to the door. If he made it out, Gram would be gone.

Deanna found her voice. "No!"

The same rancher that had warned them to be quiet before turned to face her, red faced. "That's it!" he said.

Deanna pushed past him. She couldn't let Greg make it any farther.

"Deanna, wait!" Sean called after her. She didn't stop until she was standing in front of the sheriff.

Hundreds of eyes watched her. She sensed the reporters' curiosity and heard frantic clicks of cameras. A stunned silence settled over the bleachers as everyone leaned forward in their seats, fascinated by the crazy woman interrupting the meeting. She'd probably end up on the news, but all she cared about was getting Gram away from that gun. Greg was almost to the door.

"What is—" Sheriff Johnson started to say.

"Greg Martin," Deanna shouted, pointing to Gram. "We all see you, Greg. Let her go."

The sheriff's head snapped in the direction she pointed.

Deanna kept speaking, determined to draw all eyes onto Greg. It was a risk, but it was all she could think to do. "It's Greg Martin. You all see him, right? It's Greg Martin," she yelled. She wanted him to know he'd been identified, to make him feel vulnerable. "You won't shoot her with all these witnesses, will you, Greg?"

"Gun!" someone from the bleachers shrieked.

Chaos erupted. Reporters ran for cover. The clang of their crashing metal chairs echoed across the gym and mixed with the heavy pounding of stampeding feet on the bleachers. Women screamed, men shouted, kids cried.

Sheriff Johnson fixed his firearm on Greg. "Drop it, Martin!" he commanded.

Greg shoved Gram away from him, sending her sprawling across the floor before he slammed his body against the crash bar on the door and disappeared into the night, deputies following quickly on his heels. Deanna sprinted and collapsed onto her hands and knees in front of Gram.

"Are you all right?"

Tears flowed as she put her palms on Gram's cheeks, searching her grandmother's eyes for the answer to her question.

Gram was pale and shaking, but Deanna

didn't see any injuries as she helped her to her feet. She gripped Gram's shoulders and pulled her into a desperate hug. Deanna sobbed, forgetting she should be ashamed of her public display of emotion.

"Thank You, God. Thank You, God," she cried. Soon it was Gram who was comforting her. Gram smoothed back Deanna's hair and let her bawl on her shoulder.

Deanna swiped at her running nose. "Why did Greg bring you here?"

"He didn't. I was already here."

"But The Hangar was broken into. I thought you'd been kidnapped."

Gram shook her head. "No, I closed early so I could come to hear what the sheriff had to say. I had just stepped down from the bleachers to use the bathroom when he snuck up behind me and shoved that gun in my back."

"I was so worried, Gram."

"I'm okay," Gram assured her. "But what did he want from me?"

Deanna squeezed her arms around Gram even tighter. She'd explain in a minute. Somewhere out there, vicious men waited, determined to shut Deanna up, to kill her if they could, but she and Sean had defied them so far. They were all still alive. Gram was safe. At the moment that was all that mattered.

* * *

Sean held his throbbing head in his hands. A rock-hard goose egg had grown where Nathan Reid's shotgun had connected with his skull. Would this day ever end?

Sean couldn't decide if Deanna was the bravest person he knew or just the most impulsive. He supposed the right label for her all depended on the outcome, and in this case, the outcome had been very good. Sean never would have thought to call Greg Martin out like that. Putting him in the spotlight was gutsy, stupid yet brilliant, all at the same time.

Sheriff Johnson joined him. "You know what all of that was about?"

Sean gave his friend a lopsided grin. "I've got a long story for you."

"I was afraid of that." Jim pinched the bridge of his nose and closed his eyes. "Give me a chance to take care of this media mess first. Then I'll meet you out front. You can fill me in then."

Jim nodded his head toward Deanna. "That was quite a show she put on for us."

Sean chuckled but there was no joy in it. "Yeah. She doesn't do anything halfway," he said. Why did he sound so bitter? Shouldn't he be celebrating with her?

"She's got guts—you have to give her that much," Jim said.

"More than anyone I know," Sean said. He'd always known Deanna was a spitfire—he liked that about her. So why did it bother him so much to hear Jim say it about her?

"It could have backfired," Jim said. "We could have ended up with a hostage situation or worse."

"I doubt she was thinking that far ahead," Sean said, looking at Deanna hugging her grandmother. "She just did what she had to in the moment."

More than he did. While he was still running scenarios through his head, she had followed her gut. And now her grandmother was safe in her arms because she hadn't hesitated. Because she hadn't allowed Sean or anyone else to stop her. That was a good thing, right?

Jim placed a sympathetic hand on Sean's shoulder. Someone called the sheriff's name. He frowned. "This might take a while. See you out front in a bit."

Then he sauntered off, leaving Sean to figure out the inner workings of his heart all on his own.

They were waiting on Sheriff Johnson again. But it didn't matter. Deanna squeezed Gram's hand. She could be patient this time around.

It was getting late. Ash fell in the glow of the streetlamp, floating slowly down like dry snow-flakes until they lit softly on hair and shoulders. As long as Deanna didn't think about the angry flames causing it, the scene looked peaceful, beautiful even. But it was deceptive. Sheriff Johnson's warnings echoed through her mind. He said if they didn't have to be in town, they should get out. Did Deanna have to be here? Did Gram?

For weeks, she'd ignored everyone's fire talk, figuring she'd pay attention when she had to, but Sheriff Johnson had been so insistent to-night. Was it time to pack up? But how could she leave town now when so many things tied her down here? Leaving would equal giving up. Was she ready to give up?

Deanna lifted her head and let the flakes fall on her face. She couldn't think negative thoughts right now. Not yet, anyway. All she wanted was a few minutes to enjoy Gram's res-cue, to be at peace and to celebrate. All the negativity was draining away the joy she'd felt. She squeezed Gram's soft, wrinkly hand once again. She didn't ever want to let go. She'd tell her story to the police and then she and Gram would be on their way home. Deanna just wanted to call this horrible day over and get some sleep.

Then what? Fear reached out from the periphery of her mind and clawed at her thoughts. How would she keep Gram safe once they were home?

Austin had said that they had nothing to worry about, that the key players were already in jail, so they were safe. If that was true, why had Greg Martin been there trying to kidnap Gram? No matter what he claimed, it didn't seem like Austin knew everything. He certainly didn't have things under control. Maybe Greg was the last of them. But then again, maybe not.

The person behind all of this could be anyone in town. For all she knew, it could be Sheriff Johnson himself. An image of that Jeep she saw in the meadow popped up in her mind. How was she supposed to trust anyone?

Sean leaned against the wall with his hands shoved deep into his pockets, making his shoulder muscles pull tight against his black T-shirt. With the flakes falling on him, he was a picture of peace and strength.

I can trust him.

The thought landed in her mind as lightly as one of the ash flakes, but the truth of it slammed against her. She couldn't recall ever thinking that about a man before, not even her own father. How could you ever really know if you could trust someone? And how could she know that about Sean in less than a day?

But she did know it. It wasn't like she'd figured out this monumental truth in the course of one afternoon. It was just that the day's events had revealed what she already knew to be true. Sean Loomis was trustworthy. She could count on him.

On the ride back to town, she'd questioned why they needed to stick together. She'd contemplated splitting up from him and going alone. That wasn't an option for her anymore. They needed to stay a team. She thought about Sue Lloyd's worry that the fire would spread to Sean's place. Deanna had seen the same worry reflected in Sean's face. He'd known that was a possibility when he left the crash site. He'd chosen to go to town anyway, to report the fire and help her find Gram. Who knew what was happening back at his ranch right now? What had Deanna ever done to deserve that kind of loyalty?

And that's when the plan fell into place for her. She had one more responsibility to take care of, and then after that, it would be Sean's turn. She owed him so much. They'd make sure his ranch was safe. They'd figure out how to stop whoever was after them. And they'd do it together. No more flying solo. She already knew that was what Sean wanted. Now she knew that she wanted it, too. No matter how much it scared her to need someone else like this, she would stick with Sean. She didn't want to think about it, but there was probably more danger coming. She knew she couldn't do this alone and who better to have as your friend than Sean?

"You okay?" he asked.

She dropped Gram's hand and closed the gap between them. She reached up and brushed away an ash flake on his forehead. Her breath hitched as she became so very aware of how close they stood to each other. "There, that's better."

"Thanks," he said, his voice deep, rough.

She opened her mouth to confess what she'd been thinking, but her tongue was tied. She swallowed. How could she tell him how much she trusted him without it coming out sappy or flirty? She wanted to tell him she planned to stick by him until this was all resolved, but she could imagine the "you two are so cute" expression on Gram's face behind her. Deanna wasn't ready to put her true thoughts to words, especially not with Gram listening. She needed to sort through them first. She would tell him later, when they didn't have an audience.

"Thank you for getting me here. If you hadn't

convinced me to come to the meeting and stay here, I would have missed Gram," Deanna said. "It would have been too late."

An expression she couldn't read skirted across Sean's face. Frustration? "It wasn't me that saved her," he said. "I almost stopped you."

He looked like he wanted to say more, almost like he was a little mad at her. Maybe she was wrong about what he wanted after all. Maybe he was tired of babysitting her. She opened her mouth, but Sheriff Johnson joined them and Sean turned his attention to him instead.

The sheriff's shoulders were slumped. Deanna could read exhaustion written all over him, but he planted his feet shoulder width apart and took on the typical cop stance, preparing to shoulder their stories anyway.

"You look beat, Sheriff," Deanna said.

"Nothing a pot of coffee won't fix. Now tell me this story."

Her own posture drooped. Normally, she'd insist they move this meeting to The Hangar. The condition they'd left it in flooded her mind, but she had to shake away her thoughts. She'd deal with them later. She wasn't ready to move out of the denial stage. It seemed to be working fine for now. Sheriff Johnson probably didn't have any extra time to stop for a cup of coffee anyway.

"We've had quite an afternoon," Sean told him and then launched into their story.

Somewhere behind Deanna, an accelerating engine whined. The noise made it hard to focus on what Sean was saying. She tried to ignore it. She wanted to hear everything, to make sure he didn't leave out any critical details like he'd done earlier with Austin. Instead her attention kept turning to some hotshot revving his truck engine and squealing his tires.

The engine noise increased in pitch. She directed her annoyed gaze over her shoulder as an old Nissan pickup truck sped around the corner. Deanna noted the jacked-up tires, the roll bars and mud spray. She rolled her eyes. Stupid teenagers showing off. She wanted to yell at them to grow up. It was so distracting.

Sean's voice sounded as if he were far away in a tunnel. "Austin Mills told us you guys made some arrests today," he was saying. At that same moment, a masked man leaned from the passenger-side window of the approaching pickup.

Deanna blinked. Then her brain caught up with her eyes.

"Get down," she screamed.

Sean's body slammed into her, knocking the wind from her lungs. He rolled midair and hit the ground on his back, taking the brunt of the fall for both of them. Sean scrambled to cover Deanna, wrapping her tighter against him as the first bullet hit the brick wall, spraying mortar dust. It hit the exact spot she had been standing seconds ago.

Deanna tried to count the gunshots. *Pop, pop, pop*, pause, *pop, pop, pop*. Maybe six rounds?

It was quiet for two heartbeats before the shooter started again. Deanna clamped her eyes shut and curled against Sean's body, no longer able to count the bullets. There were too many. Debris flew around them as the bullets continued connecting with bricks. Sean's strong arms pulled her even tighter against him.

The whole thing had lasted only seconds. And then just as quickly as it had begun, the truck was gone, the gunfire over. Silent beats. Sean pulled away from her. Deanna gasped, but she wasn't hurt.

"Everyone okay?" Sean yelled, his voice hoarse as he scrambled to his feet.

Deanna heard the moan first and then Gram's shaky voice.

"He's hit," Gram cried. "The sheriff's been shot."

TWELVE

Sean couldn't breathe, couldn't move. What would he find when he reached Jim's side? His instinct screamed at him. He should run the opposite direction, get as far away from his friend's pain as possible. But Jim needed him.

He fell to his knees, his hands hovering above Jim. Sean had no idea what to do first.

Jim sat propped against the bullet-riddled wall. A smear of dark blood marked the path he'd slid down after he was hit. He was hunched over, holding his right side with both hands. Blood flowed over his fingers and onto the sidewalk. Sean's stomach rolled, and a sour taste rose into his mouth. What could he possibly do to fix this?

He gripped Jim's shoulders gently. If only he could transfer some of that pain into himself, to share it somehow. Sean's throat constricted, and all he could get out was a whisper. "I'm so sorry. They weren't aiming at you."

Sean glanced up at the mosquito-covered light fixture above them. He could see now the way that it highlighted the damage beneath it. They'd been standing in a virtual spotlight when that truck drove by them. Why hadn't he thought to stay out of sight? Once again he'd underestimated the threat and hadn't taken enough precautions to protect them all. He should have warned Jim of the potential danger when they were still back inside the school. Jim was hurt because Sean was naive. He couldn't make that same mistake again.

Deanna stood to the side, her hands covering her mouth. Arlene was beside her, her own hands clasped under her chin like she was begging for something. Both of them stared at Sean like they wanted something from him.

They were waiting for him to make everything better. To fix it. But he couldn't. His eyes roved Jim's bleeding body. He was a cattle rancher, not a paramedic. He had no clue what to do.

Jim's polo shirt was ripped across the chest. The ballistic vest he wore under his shirt had stopped the bullets from penetrating. He probably had the wind knocked out of him from the impact, though. It would explain why Jim was struggling so hard for breath. His right sleeve was ripped where another bullet must have grazed his upper arm. But it was the bloody mess at his side that concerned Sean the most.

"Help him," Deanna begged.

"What do you think I'm trying to do?" Sean snapped.

"Then tell me what to do to help," she said. "I can't stand here doing nothing."

Sean ripped strips off the bottom half of his T-shirt, hardly noticing the cooler evening air against his stomach. He wadded the fabric into a ball and placed it against Jim's side as a make-shift bandage.

"Here, hold on to this," he said, placing Jim's hand over the fabric. Thankfully, Jim was still conscious.

They had an audience. People who had lingered after the meeting and witnessed the drive-by now gathered around them to see what had happened. Sean resented their intrusion. Jim deserved some privacy.

"Stop staring and get us some help," Sean yelled. "Someone go into the school and find a first-aid kit."

"I'll go," Deanna said and took off.

There she went again, taking action while everyone else watched. He should have expected her to volunteer, but it was too late to stop her now.

"Be careful!" he called. She wouldn't listen. Careful wasn't anywhere in her DNA.

Sean squinted up at the light. They were still so vulnerable, but he couldn't move Jim without doing more damage or causing more pain. Would the shooters circle around the block and open fire again?

"Sean," Jim whispered, his breaths frantic and labored. Getting the words out past the pain took so much effort.

Sean squeezed Jim's shoulder on his good side. "Hey, buddy, don't waste your energy trying to talk. We're getting help."

Deanna came back with a first-aid kit in her hand and Austin Mills right on her heels. Sean grimaced. *Great.* Just who they needed right now.

"Austin's car pulled up before I got inside." She bent over and put her hands on her knees, winded from running so hard. "Here." She handed the kit to Sean. "He had this in his car."

Austin's face drained of all color. "What happened?"

Sean jumped to his feet and shoved his finger into Austin's chest. "You told us they were all in jail. That we didn't have anything more to worry about. That we were all safe."

Austin shook his head. "I didn't know this would happen. How could I know that?"

"Arlene narrowly missed being kidnapped, and Jim's been shot. Tell them you're sorry."

"Move," Austin said. He shoved Sean aside and snatched the first-aid kit. Tossing the bloodied fabric from Sean's T-shirt aside, he pressed a clean gauze pad against the wound. "Let the professionals do our job."

"Mills," Jim panted. "Let…me…talk to Sean."

"You don't have time."

"Alone," Jim insisted.

"No," Austin said. He peered up at Sean. "Look at this blood. Don't be stupid."

Keeping one hand on the bandage, Austin turned to the radio mic on his shoulder. The dispatcher's voice—Sue Lloyd's, most likely—confirmed that paramedics were coming. The hospital was only a mile away, but that ambulance couldn't get there quickly enough. Watching Jim suffering in front of his eyes without being able to fix it was too much. Sean's fingers drummed against his leg. He strained to hear the sound of sirens.

Austin must have felt the same way. "They're taking too long. Help me move him into my car," he ordered. "I'll get him to the ER faster than sitting and waiting for the ambulance."

"Why should I trust you?"

Jim lifted his head and leveled a steely gaze at both of them. Austin turned from its intensity. Sean leaned away, too. Even in his weakened state, Jim was still very much in command.

"It's an order." He wheezed. "Give me a minute with Sean. Then you can come back and save my life."

Austin was furious, but he obeyed. "Keep pressure on this," he ordered Sean before backing up a few steps. He didn't take his eyes off them. Sean pushed gently on the gauze.

Jim's chest heaved up and down. His face had become the same color as the falling ash. Was Sean pushing too hard on the wound? How much pressure was enough?

"You can't stay," Jim said. "Fire's coming for your place fast."

Sean's responsibilities at home called to him. He'd been gone all day. Uncle Paul must be frantic for help. The firebreaks were already dug. He'd done that himself with the Bobcat. But what about the cattle? Had the crews been able to get them all rounded up? Uncle Paul wouldn't wait too long to get out, would he?

Sean shut out his racing thoughts. "I'm not leaving you."

"I'll live," Jim grunted, giving Sean the same authoritative look he'd shown to Austin. "After the ambulance comes, I'll tell my deputies you're free to go. Promise me you will."

Sean hesitated, his loyalties torn.

"Promise me!"

"All right. As soon as I know you're in good hands, I'll head home."

"Lean in," Jim instructed.

Sean angled his ear close to Jim's face. The words were so quiet and labored Sean had to concentrate hard to understand.

"There were no arrests."

Sean pulled away, locking his eyes on Austin. Austin cocked his head in return, questioning. He stepped toward Sean, a look of challenge on his face.

"Are you done?" Austin snarled.

"Not yet!" Sean yelled back.

Austin threw up his hands. "Sure, why not. Be my guest. Not like a man's bleeding out on the ground or anything."

Sean turned back to Jim.

"Don't trust..." Jim started to say but couldn't finish.

"Who shouldn't I trust?"

The sheriff labored some more, trying so hard to form words that refused to come.

"Please," Sean begged. "Who's after us?"

Jim only wheezed in response. Sean glanced down at the bloody mess that was his side and arm. Blood still flowed from both wounds.

"It can wait, Jim. You can tell me everything

later, when you're better," Sean said. He moved to wave Austin back over but Jim stopped him.

"Talk to Paul," he whispered. His head fell forward against his chest, too heavy to hold up any longer.

"What did you say?" Sean leaned in close again.

"Mills."

Jim was losing consciousness. He wasn't making sense, just spitting out names.

Sean couldn't tell if Jim was naming Austin as the leader behind these attacks or simply calling for his help. "Do you want Austin back here?" Sean asked, desperate to understand.

"If he dies, it's your fault, Loomis," Austin called.

"Ask Paul," Jim said once more before he collapsed against Sean.

He struggled to hold up Jim's deadweight. "He's unconscious!"

"Get out of the way," Austin commanded, shoving Sean away once again. Austin yelled into his radio, cursing Dispatch. "Where's our paramedics?"

Sean didn't fight back or argue. He'd interfered with Jim's care enough already. He could hear the ambulance arriving and the screaming sirens of two other sheriff-deputy vehicles joining the scene. But what Sean heard most was Austin's accusing voice. *If he dies, it's your fault.*

He was unskilled when it came to saving lives. What Jim needed was for Sean to back off and let the professionals take over. Even if it meant admitting that Austin Mills was more qualified in this situation than he was. Sean wasn't deluded enough to think otherwise. He allowed himself to be jostled by the swarm of paramedics and deputies, stumbling backward out of their way.

From a distance, all Sean could see were Jim's boots sticking out from the huddle of men circled around him. Tyler Evanston, one of Jim's deputies, jogged over to Sean, while the other deputy pulled Deanna and Arlene aside. Tyler was going to want answers Sean didn't have, but at least Sean wouldn't have to talk to Austin.

"He's in and out of consciousness," Tyler said. "We're taking him to the hospital now, but I'm sure they'll life-flight him to Seattle or Spokane."

Sean tried to answer Tyler's questions, describing what he could recall about the Nissan and the shooters, but there was so much he didn't know. He made sure Tyler knew about the reports he and Deanna had written for Austin. Tyler was a good guy. At least, Sean had thought so, but how could he tell anymore whose side anyone was actually on?

"I've got a million more questions for you," Tyler said, "but Jim made us promise we wouldn't detain you. He's the boss, so I guess you're free to go for now. You let me know right away if you think of anything else that can help us in this investigation."

Sean would tell him more if he had more answers to give. But he didn't. When those bullets hit Jim, they had severed a lifeline for Sean. Jim was supposed to guide him, to take over protecting Deanna for him so he could get back to the business of saving his ranch. Jim was not supposed to be on a gurney with bullet holes through his body. Sean closed his eyes and pleaded, *God, save my friend. Please.*

As he watched the men at work, Jim's words swirled around Sean like the floating pieces of ash in the air, insubstantial and impossible to grasp. He couldn't make sense of any of it. What had Jim been trying to tell him?

Each time Sean thought he understood, a new interpretation presented itself. The only thing he knew for sure was the fire was coming. Fast. It wouldn't wait for Sean to get everything sorted out first.

Jim had made him promise that he'd leave him, but what kind of man took off when his best friend had been shot? He should be in the hospital waiting room, pacing and drinking stale coffee until he got news that Jim would pull through.

A cool hand touched his arm. "You're bleeding," Deanna said.

Sean lifted his elbow to inspect it and shrugged. "I scraped my elbow when we fell." He glanced over to the gurney being loaded into the ambulance. "It's nothing."

Austin was talking with the driver. Sean's nostrils flared. Whether or not Jim had meant that Austin Mills was controlling the drugs and weapons smuggling or that he was responsible for the attacks, Austin had lied.

"I really, really don't like that guy," Sean grumbled.

Deanna protested, "He was the only one I could find to help…"

"I know."

She hugged her arms around her waist. "Those bullets were meant for us."

"Yeah. Probably," Sean agreed.

"Are they coming back?"

"Not here—there's too much of an audience now." He could feed her a bunch of platitudes and attempt to reassure her, but it wouldn't be honest. She needed to understand just how much danger she was still in—that her grandmother was still in, too. "They'll be back eventually. They aren't stopping until they've shut us up. We've got to get you both somewhere safe."

"But we already told the sheriff everything we know. Why are they still after us? What more of a threat could we be?"

"It's hard to testify when you're dead," Sean said.

Deanna jerked. He hadn't meant to say it quite that bluntly but it was the truth. "We're loose ends," he continued. "If they get rid of us, there will be no witnesses. No one to stand up in court and point fingers. And we won't be able to snoop around for more information, either. Whoever is calling the shots, they do not want us left alive as a liability."

As long as he was being honest, he should continue. "Besides, we didn't actually report all we knew to the sheriff." He glared at the retreating ambulance. "We reported it to Austin Mills."

"What are you saying? That Austin is somehow responsible for this?" She shook her head. "He wouldn't do that to me."

"You never know what a man might do to protect himself if he feels threatened enough."

Deanna opened her mouth, but Sean stopped her. "Jim just told me there weren't *any* arrests made today. None. He warned me not to trust anyone. I'm pretty sure he meant Austin."

Her face registered shock. "No, that can't be right. Sue Lloyd said Sheriff Johnson had been out in the field all day. Maybe he wasn't informed..." Her voice trailed off. She wasn't even convincing herself.

"Whatever degree Austin is involved in this doesn't matter," he said. "Austin Mills is a liar. That's all we need to know."

"Sean," a familiar voice called from behind him.

He whirled around and spotted Uncle Paul standing on the curb. Sean's stomach plummeted. How could he ever explain why he'd left Paul alone to rescue the land they both loved? The land Sean had thought his father had loved, too, before his dad disappeared on them and left it all behind. But it wasn't anger Sean saw on his uncle's face. It was fear.

Two more of Jim's floating words lit on his mind and suddenly became solid.

Ask Paul.

THIRTEEN

Paul Loomis's black hair hung in a long braid down his back, his diminishing hairline streaked with gray. He was almost as tall as Sean, dressed similarly in Wranglers, a well-worn T-shirt and cowboy boots. But Paul's barrel chest was thicker, and his shoulders stooped under some invisible weight.

The family resemblance was strong, especially in their rectangular faces, with their arrow-straight noses and high cheekbones. Although Paul's lips curled up at the corners even more than Sean's did, Paul showed no sign of the easy smile Deanna had come to expect from Sean.

It was a shame. Paul's face had been designed for laughter. Crinkly laugh lines and well-defined apples in his cheeks hinted at what must have been a wonderful sense of humor at some point in his life. If it had ever existed, though, it was buried now. Deep lines creased his forehead between heavily bagged, sad eyes. Deanna was tempted to crack a joke, anything to bring some flicker of light back into those brown depths.

"You ever planning on coming home, son?" Paul asked.

Sean winced. "I didn't mean to be gone so long. We—"

Paul put up a hand. "You hear about that truck crash off Tunk?"

Sean's head dropped. "Yeah, I know about it."

"Well, it caught the whole hill on fire," Paul continued. "It's spreading, coming at us quick. I need your help fighting it when it gets there."

Deanna's stomach churned, and she could see that Sean's eyes held the same guilt she felt. Watching that truck explode was forever seared in her mind. She and Sean had escaped, but once again she couldn't help but question the cost.

Paul scanned the remaining crowd, looking uneasy. "We've got to get out of here."

Sean's gaze met Deanna's eyes. She could see the decisions he wrestled with playing out across his face. She knew the moment he made his decision. His face softened, looking peaceful. He was still looking at her when he told his uncle, "I can't go with you. I have to see this through first."

Paul froze, the weight on his shoulders growing heavier. "Of course you can't." The furious look he pitched in Deanna's direction stung. "Not when it's *her* who needs rescuing, right?"

She shook her head in slow motion. "No way. Don't make this about me."

The men stared each other down.

"Sean, go," she begged. His chivalry was going too far. "Gram and I will be fine."

Sean looked at her incredulously, almost angrily. "And when those men show up again," he said, "what are you going to do then?"

"I have a gun," she protested.

"You mean the same gun you couldn't make yourself use earlier today?"

His words were quiet, but they struck hard. "What do you want me to say? This is getting ridiculous. Your ranch is more important. You know you have to go."

"But he won't, will he?" Paul asked. Technically, the question was for her, but it was clearly directed at Sean.

Sean didn't back down. "Just a little more time, that's all I'm asking. I give you my word that I'll get there before the fire does," he said.

"Sean!" His stubbornness was driving her crazy.

Gram pulled Deanna back and whispered

in her ear, "This is between them, Dee. Stay out of it."

"You're asking for time we don't have." Paul's voice changed pitch, less shouting, more pleading. "You don't know what you're messing with, Sean. Please. Trust me. Come home."

"Aren't you curious?" Sean said. "You haven't even asked me why I'm covered in blood."

But Paul had already turned and walked toward his truck. He opened the driver-side door so forcefully Deanna half expected it to come off its hinges.

"What aren't you telling me?" Sean yelled after him. "What do you know?"

"What I know is this—we've got a ranch to save. Land that's been in both sides of your family for generations. I thought you cared." Paul waved a hand toward Deanna. "But apparently you've got other priorities."

Deanna's cheeks burned. She started to speak, but Gram squeezed her arm. "Hush," she said.

"He's blaming me," she said to Gram in a harsh whisper. "I've got to make Sean go home."

"This is about more than that," Gram said into her ear. "Let Sean get to the bottom of it."

Deanna's gaze bounced between the two men, trying to comprehend what was really being said through their stiff body language. Their facial expressions contorted with emotion, continually changing. She couldn't translate all that was transpiring between them, but she eventually saw what Gram had seen. This argument wasn't about the ranch or the fire. And it wasn't about her, either. This was none of her business. She bit back her words.

"How long are you going to ignore my question?" Sean said.

Paul scrubbed his face with his hand. "You have no idea what you've done, kid."

Sean stepped toward the truck. "Enlighten me, then. What have I done exactly?"

Paul slapped the roof of the truck and cursed. His angry expression crumpled into such raw pain it looked like his face was made of melting wax.

"Uncle Paul," Sean said, his voice hoarse. "Answer me. What have I done?"

Paul's voice was so soft Deanna almost couldn't hear it. "You've become your father," he said. Then he shut the door, pulled a U-turn away from the curb and drove away.

The retreating taillights blurred into a smear of red. Sean blinked to clear his vision and then they were gone. Uncle Paul had taken any chance for answers away with him into the darkness.

An owl hooted in a nearby tree. Sean heard a slamming car door echoing down the street. But behind him all was silent. Deanna and her grandmother must be holding their breath, waiting to see how he'd react. He stared ahead, unwilling to turn and face the questions he expected to see in their eyes.

Or maybe it would be pity. That would be worse.

The slimy voice of suspicion whispered accusations against Uncle Paul in his ear. Each new indictment burned like a branding iron. Sean gritted his teeth and refused to believe any of it. There was no solid evidence. Until there was, he'd stay loyal, but there was no denying that Uncle Paul knew *something*. More than that. He knew a lot. He knew they were in danger, not from the flames, but from the men after them. Sean squeezed his fingers into fists. Uncle Paul owed him so many explanations. Dropping a bomb like that and then driving away without explaining himself had been a cheap shot.

Deanna touched the back of his hand. She wiggled his tight fist loose with her fingers until she could slip her own hand into his. They didn't speak to each other, just held hands while they stared out in the direction Uncle Paul's truck had disappeared.

Deanna leaned her head against his shoulder and a lump rose in his throat. Her touch, her nearness—it was exactly what he needed right now. She couldn't know how much it meant to hold on to her like this, to have a friend to ground him in reality while he wrestled with all these what-ifs. He closed his eyes and inhaled the faint strawberry scent of her hair. He wanted her even closer. He wanted to pull her in and bury his face in her neck, to hold on to her until life made sense again.

"You going to be okay?" she finally asked.

His face heated. It was a good thing she couldn't read his mind. He could never have imagined allowing himself to be this weak and vulnerable in front of anyone. But in front of Deanna Jackson?

"If you're not careful, your chivalry is going to cost you your ranch," she said.

He glanced back to where Arlene waited for them on the curb. They shouldn't be standing out here in the open. "I will go home the minute I'm convinced that you and Arlene are somewhere safe."

Deanna squeezed his hand. "Thank you."

He whipped his head around in her direction. *Thank you?* No arguing? No pushing him to leave? What had changed?

Her sigh came from somewhere deep. As she spoke, it sounded like she was breathless. "It's hard to admit, but I'm in over my head." She paused and then added, "In everything."

She lifted her head to look up at the sky. This admission must be killing her pride. "I've been treading water for so long, and I'm tired. It's the honest truth. I really, really don't know what to do."

How many times had he felt overwhelmed like that? Needing Dad's advice but not being able to ask him for it? Fighting to control a world that refused to be controlled. Wondering if he'd fail or succeed. It was terrifying. "I've been there," he said.

She faced him. "I'm not saying you're being smart risking your ranch for me, I'm only saying I'm thankful we're in this together." She toed the sidewalk with her boot, flicking a pebble that skittered across the street. "So, thank you."

Sean slid his thumb across the back of her hand, aware of how soft it was under his calloused skin. He couldn't leave her alone, couldn't risk someone hurting her. No matter how guilty he felt about letting down Uncle Paul or what price he'd eventually pay for this decision, he did not regret staying with her. It had been an easy choice.

"You're welcome," he said. "And I'm not gambling the ranch as much as you think. I've done a lot of work already. Everything I could possibly do to prepare. I think Uncle Paul wants me up there for moral support more than anything else."

Arlene cleared her throat behind them. "Is it safe to stay out in the open like this?"

"No, probably not," Sean said, embarrassed. He guided Deanna and Arlene back to the old Ford and helped Arlene into the passenger seat first. He expected Deanna to climb in, too, but she closed the door instead and turned to face him.

"I have a favor to ask," she said, rubbing the front of her neck as if her words were hard to swallow. "A few favors, actually."

She nodded her head in the direction of her grandmother and said, "I can't think straight until I know she's safe. Will you help me get her away from here?"

"Where?"

"Seattle."

His shoulders slumped. In the best conditions it would take at least four hours to drive over the mountains to the west side of the state, and he didn't know which roads the fire crews had closed. He couldn't afford the time.

"I can't…"

She held her hands up like she was surrendering. "I don't mean drive her there—I wouldn't dream of asking that right now. I just need to get her to Bob Salinger's place up on the Flats. He's a friend of my dad's, and I know he'll fly her out of here if I can explain things to him. Then Gram can catch a commercial flight out of Sea-Tac to my dad's base in Yakutat."

"Alaska?"

"Yeah."

Arlene was going to put up a massive fight when she heard what Deanna was planning, but he understood Deanna's motivation. Arlene didn't need to be here. She would be safer with Deanna's dad. "I know Bob. I can get you to his place."

"Once she's safe. I'm all yours."

He caught his breath. "Excuse me?"

"You got a crew hired to round up your herd, right?"

Sean nodded. "I do."

"Admit it, I'm better on a horse than any of them. I could help you."

"No doubt. But there's not much they can do now that the fire is so close. We'll probably be evacuating soon anyway. Wildfire isn't something to mess around with. Why get close to it if you don't need to?"

She cocked her head and gave him an annoyed look. "Are you seriously saying helping you save your ranch is more dangerous than what we've already been through today?"

"I'd rather see you on that plane with Arlene."

Deanna lifted her chin. "I'm not leaving town. I've got too much invested here to walk away. I can't leave The Hangar or my airplane or my horse. You know that."

"A man can hope. So, what else do you need?"

She hung her head and stared at her boots. "I can't pay..."

"Done. Next?"

Deanna's face flamed. "I'm only asking for a loan, that's all. They emptied my purse back at The Hangar."

Even if she'd wanted to go with Arlene, Sean doubted she could afford it. If only there was a way around her pride to offer her the money. She had no idea how much he *wanted* to help her. She was doing him a favor, not the other way around.

"It's no problem, really," he said. "But that's only one favor. What else?"

She put a hand on his shoulder. Flashing him a gorgeous grin that made his knees wobble, she asked, "Can we please get you a new shirt?"

FOURTEEN

The Texaco station was the only store open, so Sean filled up the gas tank while Deanna ran inside for some food. She returned carrying beef sticks, Cokes and a brown paper bag.

After distributing the food, she tossed Sean the bag with a grin. Inside it, he found a stiff orange T-shirt. Printed across the front were the words Where in the World Is Kinakane, Washington?

He turned, horrified. "I'm supposed to wear this?"

"I could go back in and get you the hot-pink one instead, if you want."

"It's not so bad," Arlene added, hiding her mouth behind the back of her hand. "You can wear it during Roundup and fit in with the tourists."

"Thanks, I guess?" he said.

Sean swapped shirts and then steered the old truck up the steep grade to the area the locals called the Flats. The actual town of Kinakane was nestled down in the valley along the river, but many people lived and farmed on this higher elevation. Deanna's house, Bob Salinger's place and the airport were all up here on this plateau. It might make sense for their plans that Sean steered them in this direction, but it wasn't right.

If he kept driving west, he'd eventually reach the Cascade Mountains. He was moving far away from the hospital where he should be sitting in vigil for Jim. And if their progress were plotted on a map, it would show them traveling in the complete opposite direction of Loomis and Callaghan. His stomach twisted. Yes, Sean had promised Jim he wouldn't go to the hospital, but when he'd made that promise, Jim was expecting him to head home to fight the fire. Instead Sean was still running away, getting farther and farther away from where he needed to be.

Deanna squeezed his knee. "Jim's going to be okay."

"I should be with him."

Sean's eyes stung. No tears fell, but he turned his face from her just in case. He didn't want her to think he was crying.

"You shouldn't beat yourself up. You and Jim? You're both cut from the same cloth. Hero material. If he were in your shoes and you were the one in that hospital, he'd be doing exactly the same thing that you are. He'd choose to help, too." Her words were like a balm, soothing. Was she right? Would Jim make the same choices?

Deanna lifted her hand and rested it behind his head. She massaged his neck, easing away some of the tension.

"He'll understand," she said and dropped her hand back into her lap. Sean wanted to grab her hand and place it back where it was, to ask her to keep rubbing away his guilt.

He sighed. He'd committed to this; no use playing the "would've, could've, should've" game now. The plan was to go to the airport first and retrieve his truck from the parking lot. They were probably on a fool's errand. The men after them had been too systematic up to this point—why would they have left his truck untouched? They had to know he and Deanna took off from this airport and that they hadn't walked to get there. Still, it was worth checking. He didn't have a lot of faith in this old Ford they were in now. It had been a godsend when they needed it, but Uncle Paul hardly ever used it anymore. Sean couldn't even remember the last time he'd seen it running. Who knew when it would give out on them?

Plus Sean missed his own rig. With everything else about this insane day being so unpredictable, it would be nice to have a little familiarity. It'd be a lot more comfortable, too. Deanna was stuck in between him and Arlene, straddling the gearshift with her knees practically to her chin. And the shot-out windows, the ripped-up upholstery, the musty smells—it was all getting old. Sean would not be sad to leave behind the old beater.

"Maybe we'll catch a break for once," he said.

The tires of Sean's truck were slashed, the windows broken and the ignition had been ripped out.

"Looks like you've got them scared," Gram said.

"Oh, is that what this is?" Deanna asked, her tone laced with sarcasm. "Yeah. I'm sure they're shaking in their boots."

She kicked one of the flat tires. Sean didn't deserve this. But what about today had been fair? In her estimation, nothing bad should ever happen to someone as good as him. Then again, nobody was asking her how things should be.

Maybe Gram was onto something, though. Sean had said they were loose ends. After all the fear Deanna had felt, it was strange to consider that maybe their pursuers were as scared as she was. Whether that was true or not, disabling both their vehicles was a practical move. Whoever was after them did not want them skipping town. They wanted Sean and Deanna stuck where they'd be easy to find.

Easy to silence.

Sean's words from earlier resurfaced. "You can't testify if you're dead," he'd said.

As they drove away from the airport, Deanna tried to lighten the mood. "At least we still have wheels," she said, reaching forward to rub the truck's dashboard. "I'd rather have our Beast than be running from these guys on foot."

The next stop would be Bob Salinger's place and Deanna still hadn't told Gram her plans. The sooner Gram was far away from Kinakane, the better, but it really wasn't fair to spring this on her. *Oh, by the way, Gram, you're leaving for Alaska right now whether you like it or not.*

Her shoulder bumped against Gram's beside her. Deanna's throat tightened. She rubbed her fists into her eyes and fought for composure. She had to be tough. Once she told Gram her plans, Gram would fight back. And that would be bad because Gram might actually win. Was she strong enough to send away the one and only person she knew with absolute certainty loved her?

Well, if she wanted that someone to stay alive, she'd better cowgirl up real quick.

Deanna closed her eyes, the loneliness already enveloping her. "Gram. We've got to talk…"

Bob understood the gravity of the situation and agreed to help. If they could only convince Arlene to get on the plane.

"You didn't even give me a chance to pack a bag!"

To say she was upset by Deanna's plan would be an understatement. She and Deanna stood toe to toe, hollering up a storm. Sean couldn't tell who was going to win the argument, but eventually, Arlene threw up her hands and conceded, "You're all a bunch of bullies, but I know when I'm outnumbered."

An hour and a half later, she was in the air. As the small plane flew away, it carried a weight off Sean's shoulders. He now had one less person he was responsible for keeping alive.

Before she left, Arlene had pulled Sean aside. "I'm trusting you with my girl. You'll protect her?"

Of course that had been an easy promise to make. Would it be an easy promise to keep?

Deanna's face was turned toward the sky,

as if she planned on standing guard until her grandmother returned. "I miss her already."

"She'll be back," Sean said. Deanna had lost so much today. He stepped closer, unsure of how to comfort her. Her blond hair almost glowed in the dark, and those sweet, frowning lips? He couldn't take his eyes off her mouth. She looked so vulnerable.

He'd be lying to himself if he thought he was really over his feelings for her. It was still evident by the way his stomach fluttered, in the way his chest ached. And this day spent at her side, working together to survive, had only made him feel more connected to her, not less. Sean would be content to stand there staring at her until the sun came up if she'd let him. He was suddenly aware of the fact that they were all alone. No one was shooting at them or chasing them. No one was chaperoning them, either.

Warmth spread through his core, and his chest and stomach contracted. She was lost in thought, unaware of how closely he studied her profile. But he was aware of every detail of her, even the rise and fall of each of her breaths. He was so close to her now. All he would have to do was bend down and let his own lips find hers. He could prove to her that she wasn't alone. Help her see that Arlene wasn't the only one who cared.

But he'd made this mistake before. The summer before his junior year in high school. One night after a rodeo in Republic, he'd thought he'd finally won her. There'd been a connection and one perfect kiss behind his horse trailer. A kiss he'd replayed over and over again for years.

The next week in school, she'd pretended like he didn't exist. By Wednesday, his dad was missing. By Friday, she was dating Austin. They'd hardly spoken to each other since then, leaving him confused and lacking the confidence to ever try again. Now it seemed as if Blake Ransford was trying to move in on her. It could be that history was about to repeat itself.

Deanna rubbed her arms absentmindedly, breaking Sean's resolve. He pushed aside his doubts and the memories that didn't deserve his attention. That was high school; this was now. They were adults and she was worth the risk. Reaching for her, he turned her by her shoulders, the heat from their bodies telling him how little distance separated them. Deanna's eyes searched his, questioning him without words.

"Are you cold?" he asked.

"Not at all," she whispered.

He hesitated for only a second, looking for permission. When she closed her eyes and tilted her head up, he stopped thinking. It didn't matter if it was the right thing to do anymore. The moment he'd dreamed about since he was seventeen had finally arrived.

Sean leaned forward and kissed his golden girl.

Deanna's chest ached from the sweetness of Sean's kiss. She melted against him, and all the loneliness evaporated. For a moment she forgot about everything except how good it felt to have his strong hand cradling her head, his fingers entwined in her hair and his warm lips brushing hers.

She could feel the intensity he held at bay, handling her as if she were the most precious thing in the world, something he treasured. She should be treating him the same way. This was a mistake.

Her mind screamed at her to stop this, to pull away and talk some sense into him. She knew better than to think she had something to offer a man like Sean long term. It was just a kiss, but Deanna knew Sean was the loyal, committed kind of guy. And she'd hurt him once—she'd do it again.

It was something Deanna had tried to explain to Gram. Before Gram climbed into Bob's airplane, she had nodded her head toward where Sean and Bob stood making final arrangements for her trip. "He's a keeper, Deanna. You should hold on tight to that boy."

"Why? So I can break his heart?"

Gram looked puzzled. "Why would you do that?"

"Because that's what we do, isn't it? No one in this family has any staying power."

"I stuck, didn't I?" Gram said.

"You're different. I'm not strong like you. I'm like my parents."

Deanna's mom had been only seventeen when she gave birth to Deanna. She'd been working in the canneries, doing any odd job she could find to earn her way out of Alaska and the poverty that held her there. She was close to making her big escape the day Tony Jackson swept into her life and ruined it. Deanna had been only a month old when Mom dumped her off with her father. "I can't do this," she'd said and then left.

And Dad? If he had to stick around in Kinakane any longer than two weeks, he started pacing by the front door.

That was the legacy they'd passed on to Deanna. There was plenty of evidence to show she was made from the same stuff, too. She'd been freaked out by her strong feelings for Sean after he kissed her in high school, and then when his dad disappeared, she hadn't known how to help, so she'd abandoned him when he needed a friend the most. That's what she did. Whenever life got complicated, she jumped in her airplane and flew away just like her dad always did. Hadn't she done that very thing to Blake Ransford just this morning?

Gram had cupped Deanna's cheek. "You haven't had the best examples to teach you this, honey, but you need to understand that this staying power you're talking about isn't inherited. It's decided."

"I'd only hurt him."

"Choose not to, then." Gram had said it as if it were the easiest thing in the world.

What if it really was that easy? Decide not to hurt him and you won't? Right now, feeling Sean's arms wrap around her, she never wanted these kisses to end. She wanted to hold on tight. She wanted to decide to keep him. But she was so afraid.

Deanna pulled back. "What are you doing, Loomis?"

His smile was lazy as he tucked a piece of hair behind her ear. "It's not obvious?"

"I'm no good at this," she said.

"I disagree," he whispered in her ear and then kissed her cheekbone.

She held him back at arm's length. "I mean it. I don't have the best track record when it comes to relationships. You know that better than anyone."

"I seem to recall some talk about fools earlier today up in your plane," he said.

"Like fools rush in?" she asked.

"No," he said. "Like fools play it safe and miss out."

Deanna rested her forehead against his strong chest and sighed. He was so solid. So good. And she was out of excuses. "Well, then, don't ever say I didn't warn you."

FIFTEEN

Back in the Beast, Sean pulled at his new shirt's too-tight collar. It was made from scratchy, unlaundered material. He looked ridiculous in it, but in the big scope of things, he didn't mind a beat-up truck and a silly tourist T-shirt. He had Deanna beside him, and they were finally heading in the right direction: *home*.

His shoulders relaxed. He could breathe easier. There was still plenty to worry about. But the memory of kissing Deanna and the knowledge that she was coming home with him to the ranch gave him peace. He wouldn't have to guess if she was safe. He would know it.

Now if he could keep his mind on the road and off how much he wanted to kiss her again.

And again.

A few minutes later he turned the Beast into her driveway and parked in front of the doublewide trailer she shared with Arlene. Deanna would pack a bag and feed and water her horse, Star, for the night, and then they could finally get out of town so he could fulfill his promise to Uncle Paul. He would get there before the flames did.

Sean grinned as he turned off the ignition. Things were turning around. It was about time.

Deanna fiddled with her seat belt and then kissed Sean on the cheek. "This shouldn't take long," she said.

But movement outside the truck caught Sean's eye. His internal radar pricked.

"You expecting someone?" he asked. He squinted into the darkness where the truck's headlights illuminated a dark figure sitting on the front porch. "Get your gun out."

Sean went to put the truck in Reverse, but he recognized the man waiting. Blake Ransford stood up to his regal height and set his Stetson on his head. He lifted his hand in a slight wave.

"What's *he* doing here?" Sean said through his teeth.

Deanna leaned her head back against the seat. "Oh. I'm pretty sure he's here for me."

The heaviness returned to Sean's shoulders. Maybe things weren't so settled after all.

Deanna shut the truck door but kept her hand on the cool metal. She was stalling. Avoiding the hard stuff once again. She'd successfully postponed this conversation with Blake for so long she'd almost forgotten she still had to have it.

Sean leaned across the seat and placed his hand on top of hers through the window. "I don't like this. Why can't I come with you?"

She let go of the door and put on a phony grin. "Give me five minutes to smooth some ruffled feathers in there, and then I'll be right back."

Walking toward Blake, she dragged her feet like a little girl on her way to the principal's office. She glanced back at Sean. She'd insisted he stay back because she didn't want some testosterone-fueled conflict between the two men, but she missed Sean's steadying presence already. Maybe she should have let him come with her.

This was getting silly. She was a grown woman. She hadn't really done anything wrong other than decline Blake's invitation, and she didn't need Sean to hold her hand when she talked to him. If Blake Ransford was making her nervous, it was her own fault for letting him have that kind of power over her.

One of her dad's old maxims echoed in her head. *People will want to ground you, Deanna.*

It makes them feel bigger than you when you let them. Don't let anyone clip your wings.

As always, there was some truth mixed into his endless supply of cheesy clichés. She squared her shoulders and called out, "Blake, is that you?"

Blake hopped down from the porch and closed the gap between them. His mouth was a hard line, his chiseled jaw set. He was a rock and despite her internal pep talk, Deanna shrunk before him.

"What's going on with you today?" Blake asked. He glared over her shoulder at the truck. "Are you still with Loomis?"

"I'm sorry about missing our...meeting," she stammered, unable to bring herself to say *date*. Although she knew that's what it had been to him.

He held up a hand and silenced her. He stepped closer and placed a hand on her shoulder. Leaning in, he said in a soft voice, "That's not what I meant, Deanna."

She'd expected anger, but Blake's voice was low and kind. Sweet. He reached for one of her hands and held it lightly. Even in the dim porch light, she could see the clear blue of his eyes as they searched hers.

"Are you okay?"

She blinked back tears. She pulled her hand

back and squared her shoulders again. "It's been a rough day, but I'm handling it."

"Come here," he said. He slipped an arm around her shoulders and his cologne went straight to her head. The scent wasn't overwhelming, nor was it understated, either. It was the perfect amount, as if it emanated from Blake naturally. If confidence had a smell, this was it, and the bottle of the stuff had probably cost him more than she would pay for a piece of furniture. Deanna was keenly aware of her sticky, sweaty skin and her dust-covered clothing. It really had been a long day.

Blake led her toward her front door. He cleared his throat. "There's something you need to see."

"Let me guess," she answered in monotone. "Someone broke in."

Blake stiffened and stopped walking. "You've been home already?"

"I've seen their handiwork all day—the coffee shop, Sean's truck. I can only imagine what it looks like in there."

"Who did it?"

"Long story."

The feel of Sean's kiss lingered on her lips, and Blake's arm around her shoulders felt wrong. What did this look like from Sean's vantage point? She wriggled free and tipped the potted plant by the door. Her spare key was gone. "Have you been inside?"

"Yes," Blake said without apology. He held out the key and said, "I was worried about you. And I went to the barn and took care of Star for you while I waited, too. He was hot, so I hosed him down."

"Oh, okay," she said, putting the key back in its hiding place. "Thank you."

She thought of her sweet horse. She longed to lean against Star's back, to inhale his leathery comfort. To let her mind go as she groomed him for the night, releasing more stress with every brushstroke. But Blake had done it all for her already.

Because he was her landlord, this was technically his property. He even owned Star. Another of their many arrangements. Deanna earned the use of the horse and a trailer for her rodeos in exchange for Star's upkeep and training.

Deanna sighed. For someone who cherished her freedom and independence as much as she claimed to, she sure was dependent on Blake Ransford. How had that happened? She'd met Blake at another friend's barbecue several years ago. She'd known all about Blake, the town's football star who had played for the University of Washington, but it was his first introduction to her. After that, their business dealings had evolved slowly over the years. With all of his real estate success and expertise, Blake had been a lot of help to her, but they obviously needed to set some new boundaries now.

She cast one more quick glance back at the Beast before she reached her shaking hand toward the doorknob. Sean should be here walking through this door with her, helping her face the disaster on the other side. He'd been such a comfort at The Hangar. She turned back, ready to wave him in, but Blake's broad chest blocked her.

"Here, let me."

He reached over her head and pushed against the unlocked door, shoving debris out of the way as the door swung open.

Unshed tears blurred her vision as she looked inside. The destruction wasn't a surprise. She'd expected it, but it still hurt. She and Gram didn't own much, but what they had either held sentimental value or had been earned by a lot of hard work. It was all in shambles before her now, reduced to a pile of garbage, a match to the coffee shop.

She swiped at the escaping tears quickly before Blake saw her weakness. "That's what I expected," she whispered.

"This is unacceptable," Blake said, his voice

granite hard. His anger was palpable. He squeezed her shoulder. "I'll fix this, Deanna. It will be as if it never happened. You'll see."

He turned her around by the shoulders. "I'll take care of you."

His words vibrated through her, reaching the lonely little girl buried deep. She'd been struggling to keep afloat for so long. If she stopped fighting his advances, Blake had the means to *truly* take care of her, and Gram, too. He could provide a lifestyle she could only imagine. He was offering a security she'd craved for so long. She didn't love him. Did that matter? Yes, it did.

"I appreciate your help, Blake, but I'm okay."

"The evidence says otherwise," he said and began listing all of the ways she was struggling. He would know. He was financing most of it. He pointed his thumb over his shoulder. "Men like Loomis? They are a dime a dozen in this town, Deanna."

Blake grabbed her hand again and gently played with her fingers. "He can't give you the life you deserve. Not like I can."

"Sean and I aren't together," Deanna protested, blushing.

Blake grinned. "Glad to hear it. So you won't mind me telling him he can take off, that I can take over from here?"

"No!"

The force of her protest startled them both. Blake frowned, his demeanor hardening. "I see."

Deanna scrambled to smooth it over. "Sean and I have some unfinished business, is all," she said. "We've been through a lot together today."

Blake wrapped his muscular arms around her, pulling her in tight. His breath was warm against her hair, leaving her dizzy, claustrophobic. "Yeah, well, you and I have some unfinished business, too, don't we?"

She pushed her forearms against his chest, fighting for extra space. "You're hurting me, Blake. Let go."

"I think I've been patient long enough, Deanna," he said into her ear.

She tried to pull away again, but he held her even tighter. Her pulse accelerated. She tried to scream for Sean, but Blake clasped a firm hand across her mouth, stifling the words.

The cologne she'd admired earlier was suffocating her now. "What do you want from me?" she said through his fingers.

"Him or me?" Blake's voice was thick with emotion, hardly above a whisper, but the icy chill it sent through her was powerful.

"I told you, we aren't seeing each other."

"Enough!" Blake yanked her hair hard, forcing her face up to make eye contact. The soft blue of his eyes darkened as his pupils dilated. He spoke through gritted teeth. "I've offered you the world twice now. This is the last time I ask."

He shoved her away from him and crossed his arms. She moved to run, but he blocked her escape.

"Sean! Help me!"

"He can't hear you in here."

Her whole body trembled. "How dare you!"

He chuckled. "I'm not going to let you run away from me. After all I've given you, you owe me the words at least. You can accept my generous offer or if you think he's better suited for the job, let Loomis try to protect you," he said, pronouncing Sean's name with a hiss.

Blake held out his hands, palms up like a scale. "So what's it going to be? Him or me?"

She saw it all. Everything she'd gain if she could only say yes to him, if she chose to ignore how rough and cruel he'd just been and what that could mean for her future. She also saw everything she'd lose the second she fell out of Blake's favor. Her house of cards was toppling.

"I choose him," she whispered.

Blake's nod was slow and deliberate. "Wrong

answer," he said, drawing a gun from a holster on his belt.

But she'd seen him reach for it and had anticipated his move. She'd matched his speed.

Deanna's own gun pointed right back at him.

SIXTEEN

Deanna planted her feet wider. She inhaled slow, deep breaths through her nose in a vain effort to calm her racing pulse. She moved her aim down to center mass and caressed the trigger. Could she pull it if she had to this time? There couldn't be any hesitation. She couldn't make the same mistake twice.

But this was Blake. Someone she knew. Someone she had thought was her friend. Someone she had trusted for so long. She imagined the bullet propelling through the air. She saw it dropping him and imagined the blood. The tip of her gun shook. She struggled to steady it.

Would Blake hesitate to shoot her? She reversed the scene in her mind and saw a bullet hitting her. She searched his eyes for the answer but saw nothing she could read. How could he want to kill her now when only last night, he had claimed to love her? Did he still?

"Looks like we're at an impasse," Blake said.

His voice was caramel smooth. She detected no surprise, no fear, not even anger in it. His face was calm, his body completely at ease. Was that amusement in his blue eyes?

Blood rushed to Deanna's face, and an angry rhythm pulsed against her temple. Blake hadn't lost an ounce of control. She didn't scare him a bit. He was as cool and confident as ever, even with her quivering gun pointing at his chest like an accusing finger.

"It's you," she whispered. "The guns, the drugs. All you."

"Not *all* me," he said. He looked around the room. "This was *not* me."

She lifted her right shoulder and quickly wiped away the sweat rolling into her eye.

"I should have guessed it had to be you," she said. She was going to be sick. "I didn't want to believe you were capable of it."

He cocked his head and put on an exaggerated look of confusion. "Capable of what exactly? Business? That's what I do best. You know that."

She shook her head rapidly. "Don't try to justify this," she said.

Blake moved toward her. She almost tripped

over couch pillows behind her as she backpedaled away from him.

"I don't need to justify it, because I can rationalize it," Blake said, coming even closer. "You could, too, if you'd stop looking through your emotion. You're a businesswoman. You understand supply and demand. People will buy drugs and guns whether I provide them or not. Why shouldn't I profit from it?"

"It's illegal!" she protested, her voice shrill. She backed up more.

He swatted away her words as if they were annoying gnats. "Alcohol was illegal during Prohibition, too. Now it's not. These laws are all built on perceived morality and they come and go on the whims of men. I make my own decisions, and then I live with my own conscience."

"Conscience," she snorted. "You sure you have one of those?" The reality of the situation dawned.

"You tried to have me killed, Blake," she whispered.

"No," he insisted. "That order did not come from me. Neither did this mess, or whatever happened at The Hangar. They didn't know how much you meant to me, or they wouldn't have dared."

They kept their guns trained on each other's

hearts, their unblinking eyes locked as they circled each other in a strange slow dance.

"Yeah, I can see how much you care," Deanna muttered.

Blake quickly closed the gap between them, backing her against the wall. "Can you even see your own hypocrisy?" he hissed, his breath warming her cheek. "Or have you already forgotten how much you have benefited from my success?"

The truth slammed against her. Every little favor from him. Every little act of generosity over the years. It had all been a trap. Making her owe him more and more until she was so far in his debt she couldn't make it without him. She would have washed up a long time ago if it hadn't been for Blake. Now he was collecting on that debt.

His voice softened again as he added, "Can't you see how much you can *still* benefit from it?"

The life of luxury and prestige spread out before her like a banquet. No more struggle. No more worry about Gram. A real home instead of this trailer. No more fighting to keep her head above water. Horses…an arena.

She felt the solid wall behind her. No escape. Her elbows were bent, the tip of her gun pushed against his chest, and still he was closing in on her. He rested his forearm against the wall above her head and his cologne's heady scent filled her nostrils again, making her dizzy.

"I can't be bought."

"That's funny." Blake chuckled low and deep. "I thought I'd done that already."

Shoot him! Her hands were trembling, and she couldn't stop them. She stood straighter, grasping for some sense of control.

"Back up, Blake!" she screamed, shoving at him with the tip of her gun. "Give me some space or I will pull this trigger."

Blake lifted his hands in surrender and gave her a little space. "See. This right here." He gestured loosely at her with his gun. "If I could only make you see our potential together. My business sense combined with your passion?" He shook his head and said in a breathless voice, "You are so beautiful, Deanna, but I don't want a trophy. I want a partner. Together we could be unstoppable."

She heard a fist pound against the front door, and Sean's muffled voice called from outside. "Deanna?"

He pounded again and again. "Deanna, open up!"

A dark mask descended over Blake's expression. He snarled at her. "Everyone has a price, Deanna," he said through gritted teeth.

"I don't."

He raised an eyebrow. "Really? There's nothing I could promise you to convince you to put down that gun? Nothing at all."

She steadied her aim and leaned harder into it, determined. She shook her head no. She would not be a kept woman.

"If you won't let me give you something, I guess I'll have to take something away instead."

The pounding on the door continued as Blake pulled a two-way radio off his belt and spoke into it. "You here yet?"

"Here," a crackly voice responded.

Deanna's pulse accelerated. She recognized Greg Martin's voice. Fear scampered up her spine. "What are you doing?" she asked. Did she want the answer?

Blake's mouth curved into a small smile as he pushed the button on the radio.

"You got Loomis in sight?" Blake asked.

Deanna gasped. "No!" This couldn't be happening. She wouldn't be responsible for it.

"Easy shot," Greg's voice answered.

Blake's gaze connected with hers in question.

"Don't do it," she begged. She didn't even try to hold back the tears. They rolled down her face and into her mouth, salty on her tongue.

"Hold for my order," Blake said.

"Copy that." Greg sounded eager for that order to come. "Just say the word. I got him."

More pounding. The doorknob wiggled, but Blake must have locked it when they came in.

"Deanna, I need to know you're okay," Sean called.

She closed her eyes. Sweet, chivalrous Sean. What would he do for her if their places were reversed?

"So you do have a price," Blake said with a sad smile.

She leaned her head against the wall and let depression's dark veil envelop her. Everything was too heavy, including the gun. She dropped it to her side.

"I go with you, Sean lives?" she asked. Even she could hear the brokenness in her voice. Blake had to know he'd won.

Blake holstered his gun and took hers away from her. "He'll get a head start," he said. "That's all I can promise."

"That's not the deal I'm making," Deanna said. "I go with you, Sean lives."

Blake patted his pocket. "Well, you aren't in any position to negotiate at the moment, are you?"

He held his hand out to her and raised an eyebrow. "Ready to play the happy couple, sweetheart?"

* * *

Sean paced. Should he kick in the door?

If Deanna didn't show her face soon, he would do it. He scrubbed his face with both hands. She'd said five minutes. Where was she? Had he waited too long already?

He lifted his hand to knock one last time, but before he could strike it, the door swung open to Deanna's smiling face. Behind her, books littered the floor, the coffee table was overturned and pictures had been torn from the wall. His muscles tensed and he was ready to fight, yet she was grinning at him as if he were a guest arriving for a dinner party. His fist hovered in midair as his brain grappled with the conflicting information in front of him.

"Sorry I kept you waiting," she said, her tone's sweetness jarring, out of place against the backdrop of destruction behind her. Why was she acting so weird?

Sean lowered his arm slowly. "Everything okay in here?"

His hackles rose as Blake Ransford filled the space behind her. Sean's fingers curled into a fist. He wanted to knock the condescension off that pompous face.

Blake stretched around Deanna, offering his hand to shake. "Sean, glad to see you in one piece."

Sean obeyed mechanically. He wasn't sure he could say the same thing in return, so he kept his mouth shut. Blake straightened and draped his arm casually across Deanna's shoulders, staking his claim. She didn't wriggle out from under it, didn't show any discomfort at being claimed.

Sean felt like someone had reached inside his body and was wringing out his kidney. The tension released and his arms hung at his side. He was such a fool! It didn't take a genius to guess what was coming next.

Deanna's face flushed crimson. "Blake has volunteered to help me with everything until all of this blows over." She stumbled over her next words. "So you won't have to take care of me anymore. You can get home now."

Sean squared his shoulders. "This is what you want, Deanna?"

"Now you can stop worrying about me," she said.

As if it were that easy. Like he could turn it off. "That's not what I asked you. I asked if this is what *you* want."

Blake crossed his arms. "Is there going to be a problem here, Loomis?"

Sean ignored him and addressed Deanna. "I promised your grandmother that I'd keep you safe," Sean said. "Are you safe?"

"Of course," she said. "You're not the only good guy in town, Sean."

"You said you were glad we were in this together," he said. "I still want that. Don't you?"

She wouldn't look him in the eyes. Sean clutched her arms above the elbows and made her look at him. He studied her eyes for the truth. "Do you want me to leave, Deanna? Because if you do, you are going to have to say it plain." He looked at Blake when he added, "Otherwise, I'm not going anywhere."

Deanna opened her mouth, then shut it. Tears welled but didn't spill from her stormy eyes. "This is what's best, Sean."

"Again, that's not what I asked."

"I want you to go," she whispered. "I'm sorry."

He dropped his hands without a word and jumped from the porch, ready to bolt for the safety of his truck before he revealed too much of his disappointment.

"Sean!"

He turned, hoping for an explanation.

She stood on her tiptoes and kissed his cheek. "Thank you for everything. Stay safe, okay?" Her eyes begged him to understand. But he didn't want her pity. He just wanted to leave and get on with things.

"Yeah, you too, Deanna," he said over his

shoulder, each bitter word burning his tongue. He strode toward the truck, too angry to say more.

In the privacy of the dark cab he slammed his open palm against the Beast's steering wheel, relishing the sting. It was time to wake up. He hadn't realized how much of a fairy-tale ending he'd been entertaining. He saw again the disgust in Uncle Paul's face, suddenly aware of just how much those romantic notions had cost him. Sean hit the wheel twice more for good measure and started the ignition. He had promised he'd go home after he knew Deanna was safe. He didn't particularly like Blake Ransford, but the man was just as capable as Sean was of protecting Deanna. With all his money, he was probably more equipped for it.

It was time to go home.

The old truck roared to life on the first turn of the key, a small mercy to Sean's stung pride. He flipped a three-point turn, spitting up gravel in the process.

He grimaced. "I am so tired of being your fool, Deanna Jackson."

Sean slowed his exit, determined to preserve whatever dignity he had left. Braking at the top of the driveway, he allowed himself a final look through the rearview mirror. Deanna lifted her hand in a small wave goodbye, making Sean's chest warm. The sad little gesture melted his anger, replacing it with concern. Had his pride made him too hasty?

Deanna's slender frame illuminated by the porch light looked almost childlike standing in Blake's shadow. Blake's large hand gripped her shoulder, possessing her. Where had the feisty cowgirl gone? She didn't seem at all happy, so why was she sending him away?

He paused with his hand hovering above the gearshift, tempted to throw the truck into Reverse, to go back and fight for her. But before he acted, Blake pulled Deanna toward the door, and then she was out of sight. Sean felt the loss in his gut.

He listened to the *click, click, click* of the truck's blinker. Was Deanna really okay? Could he trust Blake to keep her safe?

Sean dropped his gaze from the mirror. He had no right to ask those questions. Deanna had made her choice—he had heard her say it with her own mouth. She hadn't acted scared. She was a grown woman. It wasn't like he could force her to come with him. She wanted him to leave. He would leave.

"Lord, she's Yours," he prayed aloud. "Keep her safe."

SEVENTEEN

Deanna's shoulder ached under Blake's vise grip as he pushed her into the living room and toward the couch. She stumbled forward, tripping over books scattered on the ground. One of her high school yearbooks skidded forward and bounced off the sofa's hem.

"Sit," Blake commanded, pushing her into the soft cushions.

She stifled a painful sob. Sean was gone. She had bargained for his life with her own. Now it was time for her new reality to begin.

Blake had his gun out again. Deanna missed the reassuring pressure of her own gun in her waistband. Feeling that empty space where the gun had been accentuated the weight of her helplessness.

She waved toward his weapon. "I can see we're beginning this relationship of ours with a foundation of trust and all that."

If she were smart, she'd keep her sassy mouth

shut and try not to anger the man with the gun, but she could not pretend. This whole thing was a farce. How long did Blake expect her to keep up this act? Getting tired of her was inevitable. And when he did, how would he dispose of her? Maybe she could speed things up. Make Blake mad enough and spare herself the interim misery.

There she went again. Thinking only about herself. She was here for Sean's sake. Even if it took hurting him, even if it meant groveling and placating Blake. Sean needed her to buy him time.

Blake knelt before her and braced his hands on each side of her shoulders, pinning her to the couch. "I'm not naive enough to believe it will happen overnight," he said softly. He caressed her cheekbone with the tip of the pistol. "You can learn to love me. It will start slow, I know. You'll appreciate the life I can give you first. Then you'll see what I can see. We are meant for each other, Deanna. I knew it the moment I met you. We will do great things together."

Deanna deflated. She sunk farther into the soft cushions. She couldn't look into Blake's eyes, couldn't stand to see how much he believed what he was saying. She had done this.

Somehow she had convinced him she was a woman whose heart was for sale.

"You've always trusted me in the past," he continued. "It will take time for me to earn it back, but I will. I promise I will. We'll start the rebuilding process right after I take care of one last piece of business. This will hurt, but it's necessary. There's nothing I can do about it. It has to be done, or I won't be able to give you the future I want for you."

She sat up, alert. "What do you mean? Do what?"

He pulled away from her and studied the gun in his hand. "I'm sorry, Deanna. Think of this as ripping the Band-Aid off quickly."

She gripped the edge of the sofa and leaned toward him. "Wait. What are you going to do?"

Blake picked up the walkie-talkie.

"Martin?"

"Yeah?"

"You've got your green light."

Deanna leaped up from the couch and lunged for the radio. "No!" she screamed.

Blake pushed her hard, knocking her to the ground. She fell, hitting her shoulder against the coffee table on her way down. "Blake, don't do this!" she begged.

Genuine pity played across his features

before he spoke into the radio again. "Do it, Greg. Take out Loomis."

High-beam headlights lit up the cab behind Sean. The hair on his forearms prickled. Now what? He gazed over his shoulder, squinting against the blinding beacons closing in on him.

Sean flashed his own lights a few times as a friendly reminder, hoping his instincts were wrong, that the vehicle behind him held some forgetful neighbor of Deanna's on his way home. But instead of dimming his high beams, the other driver revved his engine and closed the gap between them even more. No rest for the weary. Whoever was behind him wasn't friendly.

"Not again," Sean groaned.

His heartbeat was a painful staccato as adrenaline took over. His muscles tightened, his hearing tuned, his vision tunneled. He was ready to fight. He squeezed the steering wheel tight and slammed down on the gas pedal.

The speedometer's needle was rising but not fast enough. He pushed his entire body weight onto the accelerator until it was completely flattened against the truck floor. All he could hope to do at this point was lead whoever was behind him as far away from Deanna as possible.

"Go," he commanded the Beast.

He felt the soft kiss of the breeze against his cheek before he heard the explosion. This time it was the front windshield that was hit, the glass splintering in front of him. More bullets zipped through the glassless back window, just missing Sean's head. His pulse thundered. He was too exposed. Lit up from behind like this, he imagined his silhouette was one of those black outlines on a shooting-range target. The cab filled with more bullets, more confusion and noise.

White pain erupted across his vision. Sean slapped his hand against his ear, desperate to push away the searing burn. He groaned and patted around the side of his head, relieved to find his ear still attached. So much pain and blood for just a nick!

The sickening crunch of folding metal filled the cab. The other truck had made contact, ramming him from behind. Time stretched as Sean's body whiplashed in slow motion.

Then the motion stopped suddenly, leaving a heavy silence. The collision had felt slow but had actually happened so fast.

Sean panted, wiping his slippery hands on his jeans. He gripped the wheel like a lifeline, waiting for his scrambled brain to assess the situation. It had been a hard hit, but he was fine and the motor was still running. He looked backward and saw the front grill of a white Tundra backing away, preparing for another run at him.

Sean slammed the accelerator, adrenaline pushing away all of the aches and pains.

A stop sign loomed ahead. He ran it and at the last possible second swung the truck into a right turn. He wrestled to maneuver the turn without the help of power steering, narrowly missing a tumble down an embankment into the orchard beside him.

The Tundra executed the turn with ease and pulled parallel to Sean. Robinson Canyon Road had only a mile or so to go before it would live up to its name, dramatically dropping into the canyon that led from the Flats down to the sleepy town in the valley below.

Sean twisted, trying to see the other driver through the tinted glass.

"Are you insane?" he yelled above the roar of the wind and dueling motors. They couldn't maintain this side-by-side position or these high speeds if they were both going to survive the S curves ahead.

It was too dark to see the driver through the tinted glass, but recognition dawned anyway. In a town as small as Kinakane, brand-new trucks stood out. Especially foreign makes like this one. A Dodge? A Chevy? Plenty of those around, but drive a brand-new tricked-out Toyota through Main Street and people would look. Sean knew who was driving this one and he knew the supplemental income that allowed him to afford it.

Greg Martin.

The passenger window lowered, giving Sean only moments to duck before his own side window shattered. Glass shards bit into his skin. He heard the high-pitched squeal of scraping metal on metal as Greg rammed the Tundra into the old pickup over and over again, pushing Sean off the road and into the adjacent orchard.

He was going to crash. He couldn't stop it or control the direction he was heading any longer. The old Beast was moving on inertia alone.

Sean's bull-riding instincts kicked in again. If he could stay loose, the end result would hurt less. He relaxed, riding the powerful jerks and bumps as the Beast crashed down the embankment. And then he heard one last sickening crunch before the old truck wrapped around the nearest apple tree.

The guest suite inside Blake's house was a study in perfection. Thick carpet squished around Deanna's feet as she walked to the bed and dumped her bag on top of the silky linens, wrinkling them. A tiny bit of satisfaction mo-

mentarily broke through her grief at the sight
of her dingy belongings ruining the spotless
ambiance.

Blake leaned against the door frame and
crossed his thick arms across his chest. His
glacial eyes narrowed. He looked like an Arc-
tic wolf tracking her every move.

A muscle flexed in his forearm. No one
could deny that Blake Ransford was an attrac-
tive man. His appearance demanded respect,
even Deanna's. It was part of what made him
such a powerful influence in town. His allure
was cold in the same way that someone might
call a marble sculpture beautiful. His athletic
physique was flawless, chiseled, the type of
body earned in a climate-controlled gym.

Too perfect. Not at all like the rugged build
of a working man like...

Deanna blinked rapidly. She would not allow
that name to surface. That name might crip-
ple her if she so much as thought it, and she
needed to stay strong a little longer. She could
fall apart later.

She squared her shoulders, scanning the
monochromatic decorations. This place could
use some messing up. There was intention behind every item placed in it, from the angle
each was turned to the way the light was posi-
tioned to highlight them.

She sniffed, catching the barest hint of some cleaning solution that lingered in the air. Not the good old-fashioned pine stuff she and Gram used, but something with a softer scent. She rolled her eyes. While the rest of the town reeked of smoke, Blake's house smelled of citrus and vanilla. It smelled rich.

"What is this, Hotel Ransford?"

"Make yourself at home," Blake said.

"You're not serious."

He nodded at her bag. "Got everything you need?"

She shrugged. "Unless you have an orange jumpsuit handy?"

Blake crossed to her and cupped her cheek. When she tried to pull her head away, he gripped her jaw, tilting her face up. She clenched her teeth, refusing to meet his eyes.

"I'm going to leave you alone for now," he said softly. "You need to shower and get some rest. I'll send you some food."

"Stop acting like I'm your guest," she said. "I'm your prisoner and you know it."

"Your status here is up to you. The sooner you figure that out, the happier you'll be." His voice matched the smooth ivory of his decor, but the painful grip on her jaw belied his calm. Tracing her cheekbone with his thumb, he added, "The happier *I* will be."

Each stroke across her cheek stirred up the angry coals simmering in the pit of her stomach. She tried to summon enough energy to fan those embers back to life. She imagined swatting his hand away, pictured herself spitting in his face for extra drama. She could almost feel the slap of his open hand if she dared to do it. But exhaustion had nearly snuffed out her fire. It felt like someone was ringing her brain out like a dishrag. Her arms hung loose at her side.

"I don't understand you, Blake. What do you expect of me? Because you're delusional if you think I can love..."

He put the tip of his finger against her lips, silencing her. She was so drained of energy, felt so completely weary, he could have pushed her over with no more than that fingertip.

Blake dropped his hand. "This discussion can wait. It's the middle of the night. Get some rest. I'll be back to check on you soon."

Before he left the room, he turned.

"What?" she mumbled, her gaze fixed on the floor.

"If you really want to understand me, you need to understand this. No matter what, Deanna, I win. I always do. It's a personal rule of mine. You need to decide if you win, too."

The door shut behind him with a delicate click. There was no lock, but Blake had told her an armed guard would be waiting on the other side. He'd also warned her of an alarm on the windows and more guards outside.

She slid to the floor and lay prostrate. Pain worse than any bullet shot through her gut. She longed for Sean's strong arms to wrap her up, to protect her again. She wanted to feel his soft lips kissing away her salty tears. None of that would happen again, because Sean was gone. Blake had taken it all away before she had time to realize how precious it was. How precious Sean was to her. She curled into the pain. The sorrow ripped through her, and she didn't try to stop it.

Sean's mouth hung open. His eyes blinked, struggling to clear the cobwebs of confusion. His subconscious was trying to tell him something. What was it?

Run!

Sean scrambled to unlock his seat belt, but his fingers were clumsy and shaking and he couldn't get the ancient clasp undone.

A voice called to him across the darkness.

"Give it up, Loomis."

Greg Martin's cold tone was the motivation Sean needed to get out of this metal death trap. He wouldn't stay in here and wait to be executed. He would fight back. His eyes scanned for anything he could use as a weapon.

There was nothing.

"Face it, Sean. You are dying tonight," Greg promised. "Why not come out and make it as quick and painless as possible?"

Finally, the seat belt clasp relented. Sean flung it away and cringed at the clanging sound the heavy latch made hitting the steel door.

Greg's voice floated through the broken driver-side window. Sean couldn't see him, only hear his threats. "You can't win, Sean. You know that, right? Just come out with your hands up."

Sean belly-crawled across the bench seat. He eased open the passenger door, praying it wouldn't squeak. He held it open, listening for more taunts that would clue him in to Greg's location. He heard only the thump of his own rushing blood behind his temple. He slowed his breathing. Where was Greg now? Would he lose his head to one of Greg's bullets the minute he poked it out of the safety of the cab? He had to risk it. Staying put was a sure death sentence. Sean eased his hands into a push-up position on the ground and slithered out as quietly as he could.

The blow came before he could get his boots free from the truck, a swift kick to the side of

his extended kneecap. Sean gasped at the pain.
Rolling away from it, he struggled to stand, but
Greg's boot slammed down on his windpipe,
pinning him to the ground. Blackness edged
Sean's vision. He fought for breath, for con-
sciousness.

Greg leaned into his line of sight, his nose
obviously broken where the shotgun had connected with it back in the meadow. He pointed
the gun between Sean's eyes. "This isn't personal, Sean."

How could this be the same kid he'd grown
up with? Greg the jokester. Now the execu-
tioner? It was crazy what greed could do to a
person. Sean writhed under the boot. Thoughts
of Deanna kept him fighting. He couldn't give
up, for her sake. As soon as Greg finished with
Sean, he'd go for Deanna next. He was sure
Greg knew where she lived. Sean never should
have left her.

"We go way back. You've always been a
good guy," Greg said. He took a deep breath,
readjusted his aim. "Sorry, man, but you…"

Greg abandoned his sentence. His body stiffened. Something behind Sean's head had startled him. Greg's boot dug harder into Sean's
throat, as if he were claiming his right to his
prey from another predator.

Sean pulled at the foot, trying to move it

enough to give him some air. The black edges of unconsciousness were creeping in again, his line of sight narrowing.

"Why are you here?" Greg demanded into the night.

No answer.

"I had orders," Greg whined, begging some invisible person to understand his actions.

A deafening crack was the only answer Greg got before a bullet sliced through his chest.

Greg's eyes met Sean's, pleading for help. Sean stared back at the dying man, too stunned to move.

Curling into the pain, Greg gurgled something unintelligible. He swayed, grasping desperately for more seconds of life. Then he sucked in his last breath and collapsed onto Sean.

EIGHTEEN

Sean tried to swallow but gagged instead. He was going to vomit if he didn't get free from the dead man on top of him. He kicked out from underneath the weight of Greg Martin's vacant shell and crab-walked a pace away before he remembered the other presence behind him.

He crawled cautiously to his feet, turning to face the shooter. Who had just saved his life? Crouching, he called into the trees, "Who's there?"

Dry lightning splintered the western sky and illuminated the black silhouette of his rescuer. The next flash revealed the outline of a hand-gun hanging loosely at his side, but the man didn't leave the shadows that were hiding him.

Sean lifted his hands high. "I'm unarmed. Show yourself."

Everything seemed unnaturally still as he waited. The silent flashes in the sky marking the passage of time were the only movement.

Finally, the man stepped into sight, making Sean gasp from recognition. "Uncle Paul?"

"You hurt, Sean?"

"What are you doing…?" Sean couldn't finish the sentence, too numb to form the words. Only moments ago, a gun had been pressed between his eyes. Now another man lay dead in his place, and it was Uncle Paul's bullet that had put him there. A life in exchange for a life. Was Sean supposed to feel horrified by death or grateful he was still alive? He felt nothing but a gaping void of confusion threatening to suck him in.

"I thought you were going home." It was a dumb thing to say at that moment. Shouldn't he be saying thank-you instead? But it was the only coherent thought Sean could manage. Uncle Paul did not belong in this scene. It was all wrong.

"You needed me. So I'm here."

No thunder accompanied the white streaks of lightning dancing across the horizon. Each silent bolt became a flare of truth, bringing bits of clarity to Sean's scrambled thoughts.

Flash.

The fear in Greg's eyes when he caught sight of Uncle Paul.

Flash.

Greg begging for understanding.

Flash.

Jim Johnson's last words before the ambulance arrived, *Ask Paul*.

"Sheriff Johnson named you. Did you know that? While he was bleeding on the ground, he told me you'd be able to answer my questions. Why is that, Uncle Paul? What do you know?"

Paul reached for him, but Sean put his hands up and backpedaled farther away from him.

"Do not touch me," he warned.

Sean could not reconcile the truth presenting itself in his mind with the man he knew Uncle Paul to be. This new version was a stranger to him. The things he was thinking could not be true about the same man who'd found him in the barn after his father's funeral and held him while he sobbed. They couldn't be about the man who made the best pancakes in the West, who'd taught Sean to hunt and fish, who had worked inhuman hours at the ranch so Sean could be free to chase rodeos every weekend.

That man had been Sean's rock, his silent cheerleader, his second father. That man, Sean loved, trusted, *needed*.

"What questions should I be asking you?" Sean whispered.

"Greg Martin was going to kill you, boy. I saved your life."

"Why was Greg afraid of you?" Sean didn't

want to hear the answer, but he made himself keep going. "How involved in all of this are you?"

Uncle Paul's words from earlier at the school ricocheted inside Sean's head. *You've become your father.* Those words were the final pieces to his puzzle.

"You know," Sean said. It wasn't until the words passed his lips, thick and full of pain, that Sean knew how true they were and how deep the betrayal ran. "You know what happened to Dad."

Paul tripped back, his agony clear. He covered his face with his hands.

"You've always known, haven't you?" Sean shoved Paul hard in the chest. "Tell me the truth. Where is he? Is Dad dead?"

Paul said nothing, put up no resistance as Sean pushed him over and over again.

"Why won't you tell me? Has everything been a lie?" Sean roared. He swung a punch at his uncle's face, but Paul blocked it and grabbed Sean's wrist. He pulled Sean in close until they were almost nose to nose. "Enough," Paul growled. "I am not your enemy, son!"

"And I am not your *son*. I don't even know who you are anymore."

Paul yanked on Sean's wrist. "Do you love that girl?"

The question hit Sean like a bucket of ice water in the face. What game was Uncle Paul playing? Sean struggled to pull free, but his uncle's grip was ironclad, honed from nearly half a century of manual labor.

"Tony Jackson's daughter," Paul pressed. "Do you love her or not?"

Sean's chest tightened to the point of pain. His body was so beat up, but none of his physical injuries hurt as much as her absence did. How could he miss her so much when she'd never truly been his? Was it infatuation? Was it because she was beautiful? Maybe winning her was nothing more than a childish goal he'd forgotten to outgrow.

No. That wasn't it at all. He could see her physical beauty in perfect detail. He'd watched her transform from a little girl with missing front teeth to the knockout she was today. Her appearance took his breath away, but it went so far beyond skin-deep for him. Surviving this horrible day together had taken all of his feelings for her and distilled them down to an essential element: commitment. His child heart had decided something without his adult consent, and for some unexplainable reason, he'd been obligated to that decision ever since.

He could trace it to the beginning, back to

five years old and his very first mutton-busting event at Roundup. He'd been dazzled by the tiny towheaded cowgirl who pranced into the rodeo arena wearing a pink helmet and a sunny smile. Sean had slipped right off the back of his sheep within a few seconds, but not Deanna. She'd wrapped her skinny arms around her sheep's neck and refused to let go. He was so happy for her when they handed her the blue ribbon he forgot to care that he'd lost. When she turned that smile toward him, that's all it took. He was hers.

Did he love her? When had he ever stopped? But what right did Uncle Paul have to that answer? He didn't deserve any more access to Sean's heart. "There's a dead man at our feet and you want to talk about my love life?"

"Where is she now?" Paul asked.

"She didn't want my help anymore, so she stayed behind at her place. That's what you wanted, wasn't it?"

"Is she alone?"

"Why do you care?" Sean snarled. "A few hours ago you were begging me to abandon her."

Paul yanked him closer, his breath hot on Sean's face. "Answer the question, Sean! Is she alone or not?"

Sean pulled at his uncle's grip, jockeying for more personal space. What was his deal? "She's with Blake Ransford, all right? Is that what you want to hear? That she chose him over me? Happy now?"

Paul groaned. He dropped Sean's wrist. "I owe you," he said, his voice hoarse. "I owe you so much… Everything. Even more than you can guess at." He scrubbed at his face as if he could wipe away the grief etched there. "I promise you'll get your explanations, all the answers you want, but you don't have time to hear me out, and I refuse to tell you any of it until I can tell you *all* of it."

Sean squared his stance. "I'll be the judge of what I've got time to hear. I'm not leaving until you tell me the truth. You owe me that much."

"Not if you love that girl. It might already be too late."

Paul had chosen the one and only thing that could distract Sean at that moment. "I'm listening," he said. "What's wrong with Deanna?"

Her name across his lips took him back to the airport. He felt again the rightness of holding her, the certainty that she had been kissing him back.

"Like I told you," Paul said, "I am not your enemy. But Blake Ransford is."

As Paul's words sank in, Sean's whole body became weightless. Blake Ransford? "No, that can't be. I thought Austin Mills was in charge. He…"

"Mills is on Ransford's payroll."

This new revelation winded Sean like a kidney shot. He raked his hair with both hands and paced. "I can't believe I left her there."

He'd spent all day trying to keep her alive only to hand her over to them in the end. His pride had made him blind to Deanna's clues. She'd been trying to make him understand, and he'd missed it. He should have fought for her instead of running away like a kicked puppy.

Paul continued, "Blake thinks he's in love with her. I don't know—maybe he is at some level, but he'll always put the business first. If Deanna doesn't bend to his will quickly, he'll lose patience. And trust me, Blake out of patience is a very dangerous thing. He'll do whatever he has to do to protect his interests. If he can't bring himself to kill her, he'll order one of his men to do it for him."

"Tell me what to do," Sean begged.

"He'll take her to his place, where he can guard her best. It's that big ranch house up on the ridge on your way home. You know it?"

There were several affluent homes tucked into the hillside along the highway that led from their ranch to town. Competing for the best view of the river valley below, homeowners had grabbed whatever soil they could amid the steep basalt cliffs, but Blake Ransford had claimed the best spot. His sprawling estate on top of a high knoll gave him nearly-360-degree views. Sean passed it every time he drove into Kinakane from the ranch. In fact, he'd passed it this evening with Deanna on their way to get the sheriff.

"Hard to miss that big castle on the hill," he grumbled.

"That's exactly what will make it easy for him to defend. He can sit in his living room and watch anyone approaching. You can't drive up to the front door and ask him to hand her over. You'll have to go in on foot, climb up through the brush on the backside and find a way to sneak inside. The fact that they think you're dead will give you a little advantage but that won't last for long. If they don't hear from Greg soon, they'll be expecting you."

Paul laid his strong hand on Sean's shoulder and squeezed. The gesture was so familiar Sean longed to turn over the big hourglass of time, to rewind to the place when Deanna was safe and he still trusted his uncle. "Are you up to this, Sean?"

"I have to be."

"All I've ever wanted to do is protect you. That's what I was trying to do at the school tonight. I always knew you had a thing for her but had no idea how deep it went. That's why I came back. If I had any hope of your forgiveness, it would be gone if I didn't warn you and give you the chance to save her. I couldn't be responsible for you losing her, too."

Sean hung his head. "I might have already done that all on my own."

Paul slapped the butt of his pistol into Sean's palm. "This would never be my plan, but we're all out of time and options."

Sean wrapped his hands around the pistol, unable to lift his gaze from the weapon that had ended Greg Martin's life. What would he have to do in order to save Deanna?

"Are you coming with me?"

"The best I can do is get you there." Paul shoved at Greg's body with the toe of his boot. "I've got other messes to fix. If I can, I'll come back and try to create some kind of diversion. But don't wait for me. You get in, get Deanna and get out."

Paul wrapped his hands around Sean's and the pistol and squeezed. "You use this thing if you have to. You promised me you'd be home before the fire got there, and I'm holding you to that. They won't hesitate to shoot the two of you, so you don't hesitate, either. Understand?"

"I have to know one thing first," Sean said. "My dad. What side was he on?"

Gripping the back of Sean's neck, Paul forced eye contact. "He was the man you always believed him to be, Sean. A hero like his son." The tears in Paul's eyes shone in the moonlight. "Whatever happens, whatever you are thinking about me right now, remember that I love you. I always have, and I always will."

Then he closed his eyes and pulled Sean's forehead against his own. "I will make this right, Sean, or I will die trying."

Deanna rested her forehead against the cool window. Somewhere out there in all that blackness, Greg Martin had killed Sean simply because he knew too much. It seemed poetic somehow, that a man of such light would be extinguished under the cover of night. Poetic, but wrong. So senseless. So unjust. Evil even. And it was her fault.

She turned from the window. This train of thought was going to kill her if she didn't stop it, but there wasn't enough to distract her in the stuffy room. Sleep definitely wasn't happening. Blake knew nothing if he honestly thought that was possible.

Her hand shook as she unzipped her bag and lifted out the high school yearbook she'd stuffed inside it before leaving her house. Of all the things she could have brought with her, it was a silly choice. But as Blake had maneuvered her by her upper arm through her living room on their way out of her house, she'd tripped and spotted the book still lying on the floor by the couch.

"I want to take that with me," she'd told him, impulsively.

Blake had lifted an eyebrow but hadn't stopped her as she scooped it up and threw it on top of her clothes, zipping the bag shut quickly before she could think about why she wanted to bring it with her so badly. Her subconscious had known exactly why. There were pictures of Sean inside.

Could she look at them now or would it hurt too much? Sitting on the edge of the bed, she smoothed each glossy page from top to bottom with her flat hand and relived high school. There were too many pictures of herself. Sean had been camera shy, but she had reveled in the spotlight. She'd been so full of confidence, nothing more than a silly little fool. Her only plan had been to marry Austin and float through life on his good looks and charm.

Next to the cutest-couple picture, Austin had

written, "Hey Babe, You're so lucky, lol. We look good together, don't you think? XOXO Austin."

Yeah. What a Prince Charming he had been. But she'd bought his lie that she couldn't do any better. When the inevitable day came that she found Austin entangled with Kelsey Marquette, she almost hadn't broken up with him. Deanna flipped past the ugly memories and found the Rodeo Club page.

There he was. Sean was right there smiling at her. He'd grown a few inches and put on a few pounds since that picture was taken, but it was still him. She traced the outline of his face with her index finger.

Sean had signed his photo in the scratchy handwriting typical of teenage boys. She couldn't remember now if she'd ever read what he'd written back then. She'd been collecting signatures at the time, got his and then moved on to her next admirer. It was hard to read his message now through the burning blur of her tears. "Keep shining. Love, Sean."

He had always seen her through a different lens, saw her standing in some golden light that wasn't real even after she'd broken his heart. She wasn't—and could never be—the woman he'd imagined. And that right there might be the greatest loss she'd ever experienced in her life, losing someone who believed in her and valued her like that. It was unbearable.

"I'm so sorry, Sean." Her voice broke over a painful sob.

She'd been so blind. She had to have known all along how special Sean was—she just hadn't admitted it to herself. Probably because she'd known she could never be good enough to deserve him. She'd had a chance to tell him tonight at the school, but she'd allowed her fear to keep her silent.

"I love you," she whispered like a confession, but clarity had come too late. Sean would never hear those words.

She wrapped herself into a tight ball and ground the palm of her hand into her chest, trying to massage out the pain. It was useless. There was no recovering from a loss like this. He was gone, and he'd taken her heart with him. She'd have to learn to live without it. To live under Blake's new rules.

What would Gram say if she could see her now? No doubt Gram would give her a tongue-lashing. Jackson women were not allowed pity parties like this.

"Getting knocked to your knees is fine. It's a good place to be," Gram always said. "But feeling sorry for yourself is not."

Deanna pushed her weary body off the floor

and returned to the window. Gazing into the starless, moonless void was like looking into a mirror. The light that was so clear in Sean and Gram was just as clearly missing from her.

She heard Sean's voice. *I can't do it on my own. Can you, Deanna?*

She'd put all of her faith in herself, just like her father had taught her to do, but she'd come up lacking. "What am I supposed to do when I get to the end of me, Dad? Then what?"

Maybe she deserved to be here in this prison of her own making. Maybe she really was the morally bankrupt woman Blake thought her to be. She'd told Sean she was different than she had been in high school, but where was the proof? All the evidence said she was still the girl she saw on those yearbook pages even if she didn't want to be anymore.

She put her palm flat against the glass. There had to be a way out, a way to be free. If only she knew how. She didn't have Gram's and Sean's spiritual compass, but she did know where they found it. She dropped to her knees and bowed her head.

God, I am so lost.

NINETEEN

Sean's body screamed, his head throbbed and now he was scratched up and out of breath from his climb up the steep, sage-covered hill. At least the aches and pains proved he was still alive. He'd lost count of how many times he'd cheated death in less than twenty-four hours. He'd probably have to do it again before the night was over.

He fought the need to cough as he sucked in a lungful of thick air. The smoke was getting worse. He pulled his T-shirt up over his mouth and glared out at the eastern horizon. Dots of scattered spot fires decorated the hills below him like Christmas lights, too many for him to count. And beyond that, a stream of red and gold slashed across the top of the horizon, looking like molten lava about to drop, lapping up everything in its path, including the ranch directly below it. *His* ranch. He closed his eyes.

He should be there. But Uncle Paul was right. Deanna always came first.

The fire was so close. What if he couldn't get her out before Blake decided to evacuate them to some new location? Blake's estate was a well-guarded fortress. He'd counted two armed men patrolling the perimeter of the property, and who knew how many more were inside the sprawling ranch house? It was a good thing it was the middle of the night because the scraggy bush he hid behind would be completely useless in the daylight. He probably looked like one of those cartoons where an elephant tried to hide behind a telephone pole.

He eyed the grounds, looking for a closer hiding place. His gaze gravitated toward the stables and the darkness under its eaves. It might be decent enough cover if he could get to it without being seen. Every light in the house was on and the surrounding yard and outbuildings were lit up with spotlights. The patio door into the kitchen beckoned him. That was the quickest way in, but that path would leave him too exposed. His scrawny sagebrush might not be much, but he was cloaked in shadow here. If he abandoned it, he'd be stepping into a spotlight.

His window of time for this rescue was shrinking by the minute, and once Ransford figured out that Sean was still alive, he'd send out the big guns to finish the job.

The crunch of boots on gravel hit Sean's ears. He stiffened and peered through the bush. The closest guard was only ten paces away and coming directly at him. Sean dropped, trying to melt into the hard ground. *Don't see me. Don't hear me...* But even the soft inhales through his nose felt too loud. Surely the guy could hear the thunder of Sean's heart. Sean prepared to pounce if he had to. The element of surprise had been his friend so far. He might have to rely on it again.

The guard stopped and rested his rifle in the crook of his elbow. He was so close Sean could have kissed his boot. One more step and he'd kick Sean in the head, but he never looked down, just gazed out toward the distant lights of Kinakane instead of down at Sean.

"Better let us go before that fire gets here," the guard mumbled, but he was talking to himself. "Not paying me enough to die that way."

Sean followed the man's gaze. The molten glow along the horizon did look closer.

The guard patted his breast pocket with his free hand. Finding that pocket empty, he patted down his hips next. "Bennett," he hollered over his shoulder to the other guard. "You got a smoke?"

Whoever Bennett was, he was too far away to hear the request for a cigarette, so the man trotted back toward the main house. Sean's whole body deflated as he watched the retreating guard.

He risked raising his head again. This might be the one time all night that those two men were distracted. Deanna was behind one of those glowing windows, so close yet so far from him he could scream. It was time to go in, but he still had no clue what to do. He wasn't a spy or a soldier or a cop with a SWAT team behind him. He was a simple cowboy with nothing more than love and a borrowed handgun.

Deanna would be able to work with less. She'd proved that at the town-hall meeting when she called out Greg Martin in front of everyone. She didn't waste time with some cost-benefit analysis. She just acted.

Now it was his turn to leap into the unknown. It was like riding rough stock. He never knew what bull or bronc he'd draw at a rodeo, and he wouldn't know here what he'd face inside until he was already facing it. But if he didn't go in after her, who would?

Lord, make me brave. Show me how to get her out of there without getting us both killed.

"I'm coming, Deanna," he promised as he propelled himself off the ground. But at that exact moment, a vehicle rumbled up the front driveway blaring its horn. Sean froze at the edge of the darkness as both guards ran toward the front of the house with their guns raised. What was this?

The truck's tires squealed to a sudden stop and then Uncle Paul jumped from its cab, firing his gun in the air.

"Ransford!" he bellowed. "Ransford! I'm looking for you. Come out of hiding, you coward."

Sean grinned. Uncle Paul had come through with the diversion after all! At the sight of him, Sean's vision blurred. He didn't know if he was ready to forgive his uncle yet. He didn't even understand the full depth of all that he had to forgive. But he was so relieved for the help, and despite everything, he still loved him.

"I don't want to lose you, either," Sean whispered from his hiding spot.

"Drop your gun, Loomis," one of the guards instructed Paul.

Uncle Paul snorted. "Why don't you come and take it from me," he said, pointing his gun at the man's chest. "I've got no beef with you, Bennett. I'm here to have a little chat with Ransford. Get him for me."

Uncle Paul was taking too much of a risk for Sean to waste time hiding. Ready or not, the chute was open. It was time to cowboy up and ride this bull or pack up and go home. Sean stepped directly into the bright spotlight and sprinted, not toward the stables' shadows but directly for the house. He was going in Deanna-style.

Flee.

It wasn't audible, but the thought was so insistent it might as well be. Flee? How was she supposed to do that? She had no weapon, no escape route, only this overwhelming sense that now was the time to *get out.*

She could try to break the window, but the noise would draw the guards. The only way to freedom was through the door and directly past the guard. *Uh, hi. Don't mind me. Just going for a little walk.*

Yeah, that would work.

God, I just got done telling You I'd trust You. That I'd follow Your lead. So, what now?

God was bigger than her, bigger than Blake Ransford. If He wanted her out of here, He'd get her out.

Or He might not. Her life was up to Him now.

Deanna's hand shook as she reached for the doorknob. She held her breath and cracked the door enough to peek into the hallway. She couldn't see her guard's face, only his long, outstretched legs and the tip of the shotgun he held across his lap.

She swallowed. His posture was relaxed. Maybe he was asleep. Should she risk sneaking by him? She placed her hand flat on the door and prayed for courage before she pushed it open a little more.

That's when the yelling started.

Deanna froze. A man's voice shouted, deep and angry but not clear enough to make out the words. Then a gun fired. Deanna jumped, and her guard's legs disappeared from her view as he popped out of his chair. If he had been sleeping, he was wide-awake now. Deanna shut the door fast, her heart thudding. Had he seen her?

The commotion grew louder. It sounded like it was coming from the front of the house. She strained to hear. The shouts were muffled, distant. An engine revved outside and was answered with more angry voices. They all must be outside.

She reopened the door and peeked her head around it in time to watch her guard jog around the corner, his gun raised. For now, the hallway was deserted. She sucked in a breath, her legs bouncing with energy. She had prayed for a way out. Was this her answer? It seemed too easy.

Deanna slipped out of the room and flattened against the wall. Indecision paralyzed her. Being impulsive had gotten her into so much trouble throughout her lifetime. *God, do I run?*

She pushed off from the wall and ran for the kitchen. She cringed as her boots hit the hardwood floor, praying that all the focus would stay on whatever was happening outside and not on the noise she was making.

She entered the pitch-black kitchen and slid behind the island, panting to catch her breath. Every gasp for air was accompanied with a prayer of gratitude. She was almost out. Almost free. And no one had stopped her yet. The glass door leading to the patio was right there, her escape only a few paces away from where she hid. She popped into a crouch position, but she paused. What about Blake's alarm? Once she set it off would there be enough time to get away?

She leaned, ready to bolt, but the shouting was clearer in here than it had been in the hallway. One voice rose above the others, stronger, angrier. That voice must belong to the man who'd shot the gun.

"Where's my nephew!" he demanded.

Nephew? Wait. She strained to hear. Then her stomach dropped. That was Paul Loomis out there, demanding answers about Sean. She glanced at the door. Her escape was so close, but the thought of how Paul would feel when he found out what had happened to Sean sickened her and stopped her from leaving the kitchen.

The sound of another gunshot dropped her to her knees. She bit her lip so hard she tasted blood. The men were back inside now. "I said, take me to Ransford," Paul demanded. "I don't know how much clearer I can be."

Paul had been so sad back at the school it had almost broken her heart just to look at him. How much worse would it be now? But there was nothing she could do. No matter how bad she felt about it, no matter how much she wanted to, she couldn't protect Paul. Not from Blake's men and their guns. And not from the blow of grief that would slam into him the moment he learned the truth. Sean was dead. She couldn't undo that.

All she could do was survive long enough to find someone who could actually help them. She could go back to the sheriff's department and talk to someone other than Austin. Maybe Sue Lloyd could help her. Sean had seemed to trust her.

Deanna sprinted for the door. She flung it open but instead of stepping out into the night air, she slammed into a solid wall of muscle going the opposite direction. The impact of the collision knocked her onto her backside.

She popped back up and swung her fist as hard as she could at the man's head, ready to fight her way through the door. Even if it had been short-lived, she had tasted freedom. She would not be a prisoner again. He ducked and grabbed her around the waist like a football dummy. She pounded on his back. "Let me go!"

"Nice to see you, too," he grunted.

Time stopped. She didn't hear the screaming alarm, couldn't think about anything other than that voice. She knew that voice. And that touch. She knew that gentleness.

The kitchen swam around her. Could it be true? Maybe she was hallucinating, her brain rebelling against the disappointment of one more setback by making up something to give her hope. Maybe this was really just one of Blake's guards. He'd take her back and make her stay in that awful room again.

But no, this was too real. She was far too cynical to have thought up such a happy ending, and she didn't have the creativity to conjure up such a realistic version of Sean. Her heart pounded as she accepted the truth. These were Sean's arms holding her.

She collapsed into him, letting him hold her up. She felt warmth where he kissed the top of her head. She pulled back, needing to see his face, but he didn't let go of her hands, as if he needed to believe she was real, too.

"How did you know I was coming?" he asked.

"You're alive," she cried.

"For now," he yelled, but Deanna could hardly hear him above the mechanical screaming. The alarm!

Sean pulled her through the patio door, into the night. She tripped after him, still shocked that he was there, that they were touching each other. That connection, the place where their hands matched up, was her proof. He wasn't a figment of her imagination. He was real and in front of her. *Not dead.*

Sean's voice broke into her sluggish thoughts, reminding her they weren't safe yet. He commanded her to do what they'd been doing all day long.

"Run!"

TWENTY

Hand in hand they ran, silent except for the thud of their boots on the dry grass. It felt so right to have Deanna next to him again, to have her hand in his. Sean wanted to acknowledge it, to celebrate it, but there was no time to enjoy their reunion, no chance to ask or answer any questions. Escape was all that mattered.

The outdoor lights flooded the yard and lit their progress. If anyone looked, they would be seen. Sean hated the vulnerability, hated being back in the spotlight. He strained his ear to gauge how well Uncle Paul held up against Blake's men, but the blaring house alarm made it impossible to hear. Sean couldn't stop to look. *Trust God. Trust Uncle Paul*, he told himself. He had no other choice.

They would be spotted soon, and the bush where Sean had hidden before was too far away. They had to duck out of sight before they got shot.

"This way." Sean pulled Deanna toward the stables.

"Have they seen us?"

"Not yet. But soon. We can hide in here."

Deanna skidded to a stop. "It's the first place they'll check."

Sean dropped her hand. "Got a better plan?" he asked.

"That's your department."

"Not anymore."

They crashed into the dusty interior of the stables and doubled over, their hands on their knees. They gulped in the air, choking on the dust they'd stirred up. Dusty as it was, it was still cleaner than the thick smoke outside.

"You don't have a plan?" Deanna cocked her head at him. "For real?"

Sean straightened, his hands on his hips. "I hadn't thought past rescuing you. I didn't expect it to be…"

"So easy?" It looked like a struggle for her to not laugh. "Did I mess up your knight in shining armor moment?"

A horse snorted behind Sean, apparently annoyed they'd dared to invade its space.

"I didn't know Blake kept another horse," Deanna said. She opened the stall and patted the animal's neck. "Don't worry, buddy. We're friends." Over her shoulder she told Sean, "I thought Star was Blake's only horse. This guy must be new."

As Sean's eyes adjusted, the horse's tall outline and arrogant stance stood out from the rest of the darkness. Maybe this was their answer. The silence outside made Sean antsy. Those men would find them soon. In fact, he was surprised they weren't here yet. "We can ride him out of here."

The whites of the horse's eyes nearly glowed in the dark. Sean stepped closer. He squinted again, his jaw dropping. No. It couldn't be.

"He's gorgeous," Deanna whispered.

"Yes, he is," Sean agreed, his nostrils flaring as he struggled to contain his anger.

He reached out until his fingers found the brand on the horse's hindquarters right where Sean knew it would be. He traced the two familiar letters—the straight, proud back of the *L*, the curved, feminine *C*. His finger followed the loops of the lapped circles, the symbol his parents had chosen when their marriage united Loomis and Callaghan ranches, making them more than a corporation…a family.

He could feel his body temperature rising, his blood boiling. The next time he faced Blake Ransford, that thief would regret this.

"He *is* a beauty, isn't he, Loomis?" a voice mocked him from the doorway behind him.

Sean swung and pointed Uncle Paul's pistol at Blake Ransford, more than ready to shoot.

Deanna gaped at the two men as they faced off, pistols raised, her throat tight. Had they gotten this far to lose now? Sean and Blake held each other's lives on the tips of their trigger fingers. One false move could spook either one, and it would be over. One of them, or both of them, with a hole through his body.

"You're supposed to be dead," Blake said.

"And you're a thief," Sean countered.

Why hadn't Blake pulled his trigger already? He'd had the opportunity with Sean's back turned, but Blake had given him time to turn around, to raise his gun and defend himself. Did Blake have some twisted sense of honor? Killing is okay, but don't shoot a man in the back? He must have his own rules, the things that allowed him to sleep at night and then face himself in the mirror the next morning.

She leaned against the stallion's warm neck, breathing in its leathery, dusty scent, and begged God for help once again. She could not lose Sean a second time.

Blake chuckled. "You think I *stole* that horse. You're clueless, Loomis."

His words made Sean stumble, temporarily throwing him off guard. She couldn't stand seeing Blake bully Sean like that. It was the same way he'd controlled her for so long. Without thinking, she grabbed the pitchfork leaning against the wall and then flung herself up onto the horse's back.

"Yah!" She urged the horse out of its stall, one hand clinging to the bridle, the other raising the pitchfork like a jousting knight. Both men dived out of her way. At that same moment, a gun fired from behind her, followed by Blake's anguished screams.

Paul Loomis stood in the doorway, his gun still raised. Blood bloomed through the hole in Blake's jeans where Paul's bullet had hit him in the thigh. Deanna slid off the horse and pushed the tines of the pitchfork toward Blake's belly, forcing him farther down onto his back. Panting with pain, Blake squirmed under her. Deanna pushed harder on the pitchfork, not breaking the skin but hard enough to remind him that she could if she needed.

"Give me a reason to do it, Blake..." she growled.

Sean pointed his gun at Blake's face. "Hand her your gun," he commanded.

Blake's lips thinned as he looked at Deanna. She read it in his eyes. He was through with her. He would kill her right now if he had the power to do it. "You'll regret this," he hissed.

"No, I won't." She stepped a boot into Blake's chest and grabbed his gun. "I've thought about it like you said, and I've decided in this story, you *don't* win."

He snarled, "You've picked the losing side."

"Says the man on his back." She smirked.

Blake's face was ashen from the pain but he managed to lift the corners of his mouth into a condescending smile. "Hear that?"

Sean jogged to the doorway and looked. "Trucks. Lots of them coming up the driveway."

"That's my backup," Blake said. "As soon as Paul showed up, I called in the cavalry. Trust me—you'll never get away."

"Go," Paul said. "I've got him."

Sean swung atop the horse. Deanna handed him the lead rope and then let him pull her up behind him. She wrapped her arms around his waist and melted against his strong back.

"Hurry," Paul urged. "Don't go out the front. Find another route out."

"What about you?" Sean asked, the horse prancing underneath them. "They'll kill you."

"Stick to the plan. I'll meet you at home."

Blake attempted to say more, but Paul silenced him with a quick kick to the kidney.

Sean urged the horse forward with his heel,

pushing it out the door. The gunfire began the moment they broke into the lit-up yard.

"Stop!" someone yelled.

Spooked by the bullets, the horse careened at top speed for the ridge. If Sean didn't turn soon, the horse was frightened enough to actually jump over the edge.

"Where now?" Deanna shouted into Sean's ear.

"Over," he said.

"Over?" Her stomach lurched. "You don't mean…"

No way. Sean wouldn't seriously consider running a horse of this pedigree over that ridge, would he? What if the horse broke its leg? What if it tumbled and crushed them?

But he didn't slow down. Deanna's brain screamed to get off this horse, off before Sean took her where she most certainly did not want to go. A bullet pinged off the ground behind her, kicking up dirt, telling her the route ahead was truly their only option.

Like it or not, they were going over the edge and down the steep grade. Really, the risk didn't matter. They were dead either way.

"Hold on," Sean shouted.

The galloping stallion stretched its long limbs and leaped over the ridge edge while Deanna's stomach attempted to leave her body through her throat. She wanted to close her eyes, but they refused to shut, widening as far as they could possibly go. She opened her mouth to scream, but no sound came from her petrified vocal cords. For a moment, she and Sean were flying. If they lived through this, Sean was going to have impressive bruises around his middle from her death grip.

Sean flattened forward and Deanna leaned hard into him, fearful that she might tumble over the horse's head. A shock shot through her spine as the front hooves connected with solid ground. Then just as suddenly, Sean leaned backward against her, one hand gripping the bridle, the other raised in the air for balance. His strong legs, strengthened by years of bronc riding, squeezed against the stallion's belly, holding on by sheer will. Deanna was forced to flatten completely against the horse's rump as gravity strained against her neck and jaw.

Even for an avid horsewoman like her, this was surreal. She'd watched *The Man from Snowy River* so many times in Gram's VCR when she was younger she'd worn it out. She'd been in awe as Jim Craig rode with the herd of wild mustangs straight down the sharp mountainside. And every summer of her life, she'd witnessed the crazy Ridge to River riders racing over Suicide Hill during Roundup. Still, she had never imagined herself doing it. Yet here she was.

Somehow, this gorgeous horse was defying gravity. It didn't miss a beat, just gave into speed and instinct, and Sean didn't pull it back. There were fewer bullets now, just flying gravel and bits of earth as each hoof struck the hillside in a rocking rhythm.

The beauty of it chased away her fear. Her pounding heart matched the beat of the hooves striking the earth. Her rushing blood matched the shuddering pants of this amazing animal in motion. It was poetry. Her muscles began to relax as admiration for the horse and for Sean filled her.

The land leveled out and the tension in Sean's back eased a little, as well. She flipped her gaze behind them and up the ridge. Blake's men stood at the top, watching their retreat. Their shouts had faded and it appeared they'd given up firing at them.

Who knew how many minutes of reprieve they'd have, but for now, she and Sean were free once again.

Deanna flung her head back and crowed. "You lose, Blake Ransford. You lose!"

TWENTY-ONE

Sean glanced up the hill behind them. A few of Blake's men stood along the ridge acting as lookouts. There was no doubt that the rest of Blake's men were already following them, with more murderous intent than ever, but apparently Blake wasn't paying them enough to do it on horseback. Sean could imagine them scrambling for their rigs like soldiers with orders, flying down the driveway and taking off in separate directions in their attempts to cut off Sean and Deanna at whatever point along the roads they chose to turn. There was only one way to go. Up.

"Yah!" Sean kicked his heels into the horse's side, aiming for the next hill. He was going to have to outrun the fire on their left, but it was still far enough away. They could make it. They didn't have any other choice.

Deanna's celebration was premature, but Sean kept his mouth shut. She deserved a few moments of happiness no matter how short-lived it might be. She didn't need him to tell her that this thing wasn't anywhere near over. Deanna was smart enough to figure that out all on her own. All she had to do was look at the glowing horizon.

They were heading into more danger—he knew it in his gut—but there was no stopping now. They had to just keep pushing forward.

The climb was difficult, even steeper than Blake's hill and filled with more loose rock and scrubby bitterbrush, but like they had been all day and now all night long, they were out of options. Their priorities had been boiled down to only two things: keep moving and stay alive. Worrying about whether they *should* be doing such and such was a waste of time. They *should* be climbing this mountainside because it was the only way, period.

Once they crossed that top ridge and rode into the timberline, they'd drop out of sight and they'd be on Sean's turf. Only a few miles of wilderness would separate them from his ranch. The longing for home was almost unbearable. His chest warmed at the thought of how close he was. He was finally heading in the right direction.

None of those men chasing them could know these hills and old logging roads as well as Sean

did. And once they got home, he'd have his
crew to help defend them. If it was too late and
his foreman had evacuated everyone already,
he could find fire officials that they could trust
with their story. And Uncle Paul would help
them, too. Sean had to believe Uncle Paul was
there like they'd planned and not lying dead
on the floor of Blake Ransford's stables. Sean
needed him to be alive so he could come to the
rescue one more time.

The horse stumbled, sending a flood of guilt
through Sean. This horse was bred for speed
and agility, for barrel-racing in an arena, not
for jumping over cliffs and climbing mountains.
What Sean was expecting it to do right now
could almost be called criminal, but the horse
regained its footing and continued to rise to the
challenge. It was obeying Sean, but its ears kept
flipping back and forth. Something ahead had
it on high alert.

"It's going to be okay," Sean crooned, pat-
ting his neck. "Keep going."

They were only steps away from the top of
the hill now. He leaned forward, willing them
to reach the few thin evergreens standing guard
above them. In this high desert landscape, it
wasn't like they'd be entering a thick forest they
could hide in, but there was something about
the sight of the tall ponderosa pines guarding

the top that pushed Sean to keep going. If he could cross that imaginary line, he felt like he would be able to breathe again, maybe even join Deanna in her celebrating.

But as they crested the top, Sean's confidence faded immediately. He felt Deanna's sharp intake of breath behind him. If it were in the daylight on a normal day, they would be looking out over a breathtaking vista of hills and ravines, scattered timber and alfalfa fields for miles and miles. They'd see where the wilderness touched the brilliant blue sky. But it was night, and it was anything but a normal day.

A stifling heat and tangible blackness enveloped them, broken only by several hot spots like the ones he'd seen from the top of Blake's hill, only these were so much closer.

"It's so eerie," Deanna whispered, all the celebratory happiness gone from her now.

"It's too quiet," Sean said, his voice loud against the unnatural silence. "It shouldn't be like this."

The animals and birds and insects, the many noisemakers of the wilderness, were gone. Instinct had sent them running and all that remained was absolute silence. Sean swallowed, hard. He could hear each one of the stallion's breaths and snorts, each one of its footfalls as the thirsty pine needles snapped beneath them.

Suddenly a loud *crack* filled the air and the high boughs of the tree closest to them exploded into flame, sending the horse into a desperate backpedal. Sean's arms ached as he pulled on the stallion's bridle, wrestling with it to stay the course instead of turning and bolting back down the hill they'd just climbed.

"Go!" Deanna begged.

He pushed the horse forward as fast as he could. Had the fire line moved here this fast? It couldn't have. That was impossible. He'd seen it himself from the top of the hill before they jumped, still too far to the northeast to threaten them.

"It's just an ember from one of those spot fires. We can outrun it," he promised.

But the minute they crossed the next hill, he knew it was a lie. They were instantly face-to-face with a roaring wall of flames.

"Go back! Go back!" Deanna cried. "We've got to turn around!"

Sean spun the horse, racing in the direction they'd just come, his heart thudding in his ears. This was unreal. They'd have to return and face Blake's men, but that was the lesser of two evils. Sean feared the hungry, burning monster behind them far, far more than he feared Blake's goons at the moment.

Every direction Sean tried to run, he found

more flames. Fire had wrapped around behind them, cutting off the path they'd taken only moments earlier. That's when he knew the truth. The fire line he'd seen from Blake's hill was a completely separate fire. He wouldn't have been able to see this fire racing up the backside, because it was hidden behind these hills.

The dread was so heavy it pulled him to the ground. As he dismounted, Deanna protested shrilly, "What are you doing? Sean, get up here—we have to run!"

The hopelessness was crippling as he put his hands on the top of his head and dropped to his knees, but the worst part was the weight of the responsibility he felt. He knew exactly when, where and how these flames had begun. He'd been there to watch the first sparks. He saw again Rex Turner's somersaulting truck, watched it crash into flames as it reached the bottom. In such a short amount of time, those first small sparks that had hit the flash fuel in that ravine had grown into this enormous inferno that would now become their funeral pyres.

"We did this," he said, incredulously. "We started this fire."

"We have to run!" Deanna insisted.

"We can't," Sean said, hating the sound of defeat in his voice as he said the words he knew to be true aloud. "There isn't anywhere left to run. We're trapped."

Deanna slid off the horse and fell to her own knees behind Sean. She could see for herself there was no escape route.

"God help us," she whispered. It wasn't a command, not even a request really. She simply had to acknowledge that He was her only hope. All her big words about needing nothing but herself were laughable now. There was no pulling yourself up by the bootstraps and beating a force like this. She had never felt so small in her life.

Whenever she'd heard the stories of refugees like Sharon Grabe, they all had been just that: stories. Now that she was facing the unimaginable herself, she doubted she'd live long enough to tell her own story.

The fire's roar was as loud as if she were standing on the tarmac of a major airport. The vibration rattled her bones. The tops of the trees above her all burned and her eyes streamed with tears. She fell prostrate on the ground, searching for clean air and the words to beg God for their rescue. All she could do was whisper the word *help*. She couldn't comprehend the enormity of the power about to swallow her. Only God was big enough now.

The heat was unbearable and the visibility terrible. She could hardly see Sean next to her. She caught occasional glimpses of the horse prancing in huge circles, crying and kicking its feet in the air as it came to each wall of flame blocking its escape. She and Sean had tried their best to hold on to its bridle and to keep it calm, but it'd finally broken away from their hold, too strong and dangerous in its panicked state for them to contain. Compassion filled her. She prayed that it would be spared suffering. That they all would be.

How would she ever stand the pain of burning to death? Deanna put her hand to her chest, trying to hold in her exploding heart. As she did, her hand grazed one of the plastic buttons on her blouse. It was so soft her thumb and middle finger touched as she squeezed it. "Sean!" she said, horror-struck. "My buttons are melting!"

No matter how scared those men and their guns had made her feel, it didn't compare to this sheer terror. She screwed her eyes tight. Maybe she would die of fright before the flames got to her.

Please, God. Please.

TWENTY-TWO

Sean had failed at *everything*.

He'd set out this morning to find the missing horse and now he'd lose it to these flames. He wouldn't reach home ahead of the fire like he'd promised Uncle Paul. He would die less than a mile away while other men battled for the survival of his land. And the mystery that had plagued him for six years would go unsolved. He'd never know what had happened to his dad.

The regret that saddened him the most, though, was Deanna. Not only had he failed to win her heart, he'd have to watch her suffer a horrible death, helpless to stop it.

We're both still breathing. It's not over yet.

But it was. There was no escape. The area of the circle they were trapped in was still pretty large but shrinking fast. Soon the circle would become one mass of flame, incinerating them. He tried to separate himself from the terror long enough to come up with a solution, but his mind was so consumed with the fear there was no room for problem solving.

He stumbled forward as his empty stomach repelled the thick smoke with dry heaves, humbling him. *God, if there is a way out of this, I beg You to show me.*

There had been a similar sense of helplessness when he'd woken up in that meadow bound in duct tape. The solution then hadn't been obvious. He'd had to think creatively. Who would have thought they'd be saved by a boot string. Was there some solution he wasn't seeing now because it seemed too simple?

Scanning his memory, he tried desperately to remember what the literature the state had distributed to ranchers had said about wildfire prevention and survival. "Don't try to outrun the flames" had been on there. If he could only recall what he was supposed to do instead! Something about finding the best place to take your stand, and of course there had been the typical "don't panic" message.

The flames were closing in quickly. They needed to move. He grabbed Deanna's hand and pulled her up. "This way," he commanded. The roar was so loud now he doubted she could hear him, but she followed him toward the clearing in the trees that made the center of the burning circle. Every breath Sean took seared his lungs. It was like standing full on in front of campfire smoke and then multiplying that intensity by a hundred. When they reached the middle of the clearing, he dropped her hand. "Get down low—it's cooler."

If only he could restrain and calm the horse, but it was impossible. He could barely see the panicked stallion now, running through the haze, crazed with fear, searching for an exit that didn't exist.

"I want to run," Deanna sobbed.

"It's too late for that. You need to stay low— the hot air alone could burn us," he said.

Bits and pieces of a story he remembered hearing or reading somewhere came to Sean's mind, about a firefighter long ago who had been the lone survivor when his crew was trapped by a deadly wildfire. What had that guy done to survive? He'd lit a fire and created an area of dead, fuelless space to stand in where the fire wouldn't have anything to burn. Sean already knew all about back burning—he'd been using it to make defendable space around the ranch—but he didn't have any matches out here, so what help was that to him now?

He squeezed his head with his hands. *Think! You have to think!*

And then suddenly, he knew what to try. His

eyes widened at the thought. Could this really work? He patted his side pocket, confirming that the survival knife he always carried, the one with the built-in bearing block in the handle that he'd never had need of before, was still in his pocket.

"Deanna!" he yelled. "I need your bootlace!"

She crawled over to him, confusion written all over her. But as she searched his face with her eyes, he knew she was looking for something that would allow her to hope. "Do you have an idea?"

"Maybe. Give me your lace. Quick!" He gestured for her to hurry, hating the way he was barking orders at her, but every second was precious. There wasn't time to give her an explanation, and he couldn't afford to offer her false hope, either. If this didn't work, there was nothing left to try.

For once, Deanna didn't challenge him, unlacing her boot as fast as she could, while he scrambled on his hands and knees, searching for the right pieces of wood. He tossed a curved branch to Deanna. "I need you to tie your lace to each end to make a bow," he commanded. "Keep the lace tight."

She nodded through a coughing fit. "What kind of bow?" she wheezed.

"Just like a regular bow and arrow. The piece

of wood will be the curve and your lace will be the string. I can use it to spin another stick and hopefully create enough friction to make a spark."

"Why would you want to start another fire?"

"If this works, we're going to fight fire with fire."

Sean patted the ground, looking for a long stick he could use for a spindle. What he found wasn't perfect, but he couldn't be picky. They'd burn to death long before he could find the perfect ingredients for this task. He pulled his knife from his pocket and notched grooves into the spindle, trying to steady his shaking hands as he worked, keeping his eyes off the encroaching wall of fire eating up the space protecting them.

He'd used a fire bow many times as a kid out camping with Dad and Uncle Paul, but even without this life-or-death pressure, he'd never been fast at getting the spindle smoking.

He placed the knife against the arch of his boot, then scooped up all the dry grasses, leaves and sticks he could around it to act as kindling, and then placed the tip of his home-made spindle into the hole on the knife's handle. He lined the bow up perpendicular with the spindle and offered a quick prayer for help. Then he began to spin the stick with the bow as fast as he could. At first he was clumsy and the spindle wobbled. It fell out of the bow several times. Sean groaned. More time wasted!

Deanna squeezed his shoulder. "You can do this, Sean. I believe in you."

He soaked up her confidence in him, looking into her beautiful eyes reflecting the firelight. He would make this work for her. He tried again.

"Burn, baby, burn," Deanna muttered. It felt like an eternity passed before she gasped, "It's starting to smoke!"

He dropped the spindle and scooped up the smoking grasses into his hand, blowing oxygen into it. When he felt the heat burning his hand, he tossed the grass to the ground, then fell down flat on his stomach in front of it to blow some more, praying for ignition. Finally, his prayers were answered, and small flames licked up the dry brush on the ground. Sean cried out in relief as hope sparked inside him. He had made fire.

"Add fuel!"

He and Deanna kept feeding the little flames until they grew and spread, leaving blackened ground in their wake.

It was a smaller safety zone than he would have liked, but it was growing and it was all they had. "We have to get to the part where it's already burned," he cried to Deanna.

They crawled forward on their hands and knees and collapsed onto the blackened ground. Sean prayed the shrinking wall of flames would corral the horse onto it, as well. It was the only hope any of them had left. Deanna wrapped her arms around his waist and then there was nothing more to do but hold each other and pray as they waited for the inferno to pass over them.

Deanna rolled to her back and moaned, consciousness returning slowly. The darkness was gone, replaced by an early-morning gray. Slants of sunlight sliced through the thick smoke that hung in the air, burning her eyes and nostrils. Ash fell from her lashes as she blinked herself awake. She was like a newborn baby, not aware enough to fully comprehend what she was seeing for a few moments until her brain caught up and oriented itself. A colorless, apocalyptic world spread before her, looking like the aftermath of a nuclear bomb. Everything had burned around them, but their patch of blackened earth had spared them. Sean's plan had worked.

Deanna could hear voices and the crunch of approaching boots, but she was too weak to sit up. She smacked her cracked, burnt lips, trying to moisten them enough to call for help, but before she could speak, a helmeted man in green pants, a yellow shirt and suspenders knelt beside her.

"We're here to help," he said, helping her drink water from his canteen. His smudged face split into a kind grin. "Although it looks like you two saved yourselves," he said, holding up the bow she'd made with her bootlace still attached.

"Sean?" she managed to whisper.

"Your friend is going to be fine. And your horse, too."

On cue, Deanna heard the stallion neighing. *You saved us, God. All three of us.* His goodness had even extended to the horse. A wheezing sob escaped her lips.

The firefighter squeezed her shoulder. "Hey, it's over now. You're going to be okay. There's a helicopter on its way to take you both to the hospital, and we'll get your horse to a vet. You rest until it gets here."

It's over now, he'd said.

Deanna closed her eyes, completely exhausted. Somehow she knew the firefighter spoke more truth than he could know. Yes, the fire was over. She was alive because Sean's safety zone had held. But that wasn't all that was over.

We're here to help.

This day had been an unending obstacle course. Every time they conquered one threat, a bigger one had popped up to replace it. But now they would have help. A helicopter was coming to take them away. There would be officials who could stop Blake's men for them.

It was *all* truly over, and she felt safe for the first time. She used the last of her strength to find Sean's hand, overwhelmed with gratitude at the touch of his warm skin. She closed her eyes. She could rest now. They were alive. They were together.

And they were done running.

TWENTY-THREE

There was a light rap on Deanna's hospital room door, and then Sue Lloyd's face appeared. "Can I come in?"

"Yes, please," Deanna said, pushing the button to sit up straighter, happy to see a friendly face.

"I brought you these," Sue said, placing a vase of bright tulips on her bedside table.

"That was so thoughtful," Deanna said. With Gram gone and Sean somewhere else in the hospital, Deanna had felt so alone. It didn't matter how much she begged, the hospital staff wouldn't break HIPAA laws to tell her anything about Sean's condition. Sue Lloyd might be practically a stranger, but she was Sean's friend and Deanna was desperate for that connection, for any news to reassure her.

Sue leaned down and gave Deanna a huge hug. "That's a message from Sean," she said, winking. "I just came from his room."

Deanna grabbed Sue's hand and held on for dear life. "You've seen him? They won't tell me anything. Is he okay?"

Sue nodded. "He said he breathed in too much smoke and has a few serious burns, but it's nothing he won't recover from…" Sue bit her lip and hesitated.

Deanna leaned forward. "What is it? What's wrong?" She'd been so sure that it was all over, but maybe she'd just imagined that because she was hopeful. "He's going to be okay, right?"

"Oh, honey, I didn't mean to scare you. I just don't know if it's my place to say. But Sean's going to need your support."

Deanna's stomach plummeted, and it took effort to spit out the next question. She was afraid of the answer. "Did he lose his ranch?"

Sue sat on the edge of Deanna's bed, still holding her hand. There was something so warm about this woman. She could see why Sean liked her so much. "No, it's not that. The ranch is fine. The fire burned all around it but didn't cross Sean's firebreaks."

"That's a relief," Deanna sighed. Even without being there, Sean had saved that, too. So if he was fine and the ranch was fine, what was wrong? What was Sue keeping from her? "What is it, Sue? Please tell me."

"He's got a DEA agent questioning him now."

Deanna's head spun, dizzy from the speed with which she sat up. Rage filled her. "What? They aren't accusing him of anything, are they? Because they need to talk to me if they think Sean could possibly…" Deanna would rip the IV tubes right out of her arm if she had to, storm in and demand they listen to reason.

Sue dropped her eyes. "I'm pretty sure they know Sean had nothing to do with the drugs and weapons trafficking. That's not the problem." Why wouldn't she just spit it out already? "The thing is, the leader of the operation turned himself in. He gave them everything they need to make arrests all the way into Canada."

"Wait a second. Blake turned himself in?" Deanna asked, shocked. "Why would he do that?"

"Blake Ransford?" Sue shook her head. "No, not Blake. He's been arrested, yes. But he wasn't the top guy."

"Austin, then?" Deanna couldn't believe it. The Jeep Cherokee she'd seen in the meadow must have been Austin's patrol car. Not because he was there to make arrests, but because he was one of them. "Sean suspected him, but I guess my history with him clouded my judgment—I just couldn't see it."

"No, Deanna. Austin was one of them, too, but he wasn't in charge, either."

"Then who?"

Sue wrung her hands. "I should probably let Sean tell you this."

"Just tell me. Who was in charge? Do I know him?"

Sue's eyes watered. "It was Paul Loomis. He found a working landline last night and called the DEA to turn himself in. They didn't waste any time getting here. Agents met him at the sheriff's department at the end of my shift. He's already been taken into custody."

Deanna swung her legs over the side of the bed and began to untangle the IV cords from the bed rail. She stood up and slipped a robe over her hospital gown. She dragged the IV tower on wheels with her as she took a few wobbly steps toward Sue. "I'm going to need your help."

"Anything," Sue said.

"Take me to him."

The DEA agent had gone, leaving Sean alone with the answers to all of his questions. He'd wanted these answers for years, but now he wished he could give them back. The only answer he didn't have yet was *why*.

Back in the orchard when Uncle Paul had promised Sean that he'd make things right no matter what, there was no way Sean could have guessed what that meant. When he was climbing Blake Ransford's hillside to rescue Deanna, Uncle Paul had been phoning government agents to set all of this in motion.

His uncle had been living a lie for over a decade, the leader of an international drug- and weapons-smuggling organization between Kinakane, the reservation and a Canadian counterpart named Evan Pritchard. It was Pritchard who had hired the pilot, Nathan Reid. And it was Uncle Paul who had invited him onto their land.

Blake Ransford had wanted to replace Paul as the leader of the operation and had attempted a coup twice. His first try had happened six years ago and Sean's father had been an innocent victim caught in the cross fire. Ransford's second attempt had been recent, forcing Paul to give him Sean's horse in exchange for more time and guaranteed safety for Sean and his mother. A bargain the agent didn't believe Ransford intended to honor.

"Your uncle didn't have enough support or money left to fight him. If you hadn't gotten in the way yesterday, he thinks Ransford would have succeeded at taking over this time. He would have had your uncle killed in order to solidify his position," the agent said. "So in a roundabout way, you saved his life."

Sean was too numb to know how he felt about that yet, how he felt about any of it.

Before he left, the agent had placed an envelope and a business card on the bedside table. "We agreed to let your uncle write you this letter," he said. Sean imagined the man was anxious to get back to his colleagues. Taking down an operation that stretched across borders would be a big deal. That phone call from Uncle Paul must have felt like an early Christmas present. "I'm sure we'll be in touch soon. If you think of anything more or you have any questions, call me. My number's on the card."

And then he was gone. Sean fingered Uncle Paul's letter, recognizing the hand that had written his name. It took some time, but curiosity eventually won over his anger. He ripped the end off the envelope, took out the letter and read, "Dear Sean," but that's as far as he could get before the words blurred beyond recognition.

Deanna watched from the doorway as Sean tried to read the letter he clutched in his bandaged hands. The tremendous weight of his grief pressed down on her own shoulders.

His face was swollen and red, his skin shining with an unnatural sheen. Scratches and burns covered his body, and the gown probably covered worse wounds. She cringed, remembering how he'd shielded her body from the burning embers and branches falling on them from the treetops.

She wanted to run to him, but she couldn't get her feet to move. Sue had promised to run interference with the nurses, but she'd be able to hold them off for only so long. Deanna gripped the IV tower and prayed for help. Sean's relationship with Paul was as precious to him as hers was with Gram. She didn't have any idea how to help him heal from this kind of betrayal. All she knew was that she could not let fear keep her from him this time. Never again.

"Hey, cowboy," she said.

He sat up, dumbfounded. "You're here."

"Did you think they could keep me away?"

"I should have known better," he said with a feeble attempt at a smile he couldn't maintain. His eyes filled as he held up the envelope. "You heard?"

"Yes."

She rolled the tower to his bedside and sat down on the edge. "What will happen to him?" she whispered.

"Prison. For a very long time." Sean's gaze lifted to the ceiling.

He was silent for so long Deanna started fidgeting with the hem of her robe. She was intruding. She should have given him more time before barging in here like this.

"I still love him, Deanna," Sean said roughly, startling her. The pure, raw pain he turned toward her stole her breath. "How can I still love him?"

She cradled his face gingerly, forcing him to look her in the eyes. "Because you are such a *good* man," she said, her voice thick. Her thumb swiped his cheek. "So, so good."

He took her hands into his and kissed her palms, fighting tears she knew he'd never let fall in front of her. The ache in her chest was killing her.

"We've got a long road ahead of us, Dee. We'll have to testify. Against Blake and Austin, too, and probably even in Canada." His bloodshot eyes searched hers. "The trials could go on for months. Can you forgive me for dragging you into all of this?"

"I wouldn't change a thing," she said without hesitation. When he started to protest, she interrupted him, forcing conviction into each word. "No. I mean it." Deanna's heart pounded. She wanted to tell him everything. She needed to say aloud what she'd confessed to herself in those dark moments when she'd thought she'd lost him forever. "Sean, you make me want to stay on the ground."

She groaned and let her head drop back. "I'm so bad with words."

Taking a deep breath, she tried again. "I've spent my whole life chasing some elusive thing I couldn't define, on the back of a horse or in my airplane." She shrugged. "But I could never really outfly my life. I'm my father's daughter for sure. Whenever anything gets complicated, I bolt. I did it to you in high school. I was so scared of my feelings and then when your dad was gone…" She licked her lips, searching for the right words. "After this one day with you, I've changed. The old me would be itching to fly. I don't feel that way now, because I'm not afraid anymore. I just want to be with you, facing whatever's coming together."

She leaned her forehead against his chest. It would be easier to say this if she wasn't looking at him. "What I'm trying to say is that I love you, Sean. I love you so much it hurts. I hate that I can't take this pain away for you. And I can't see how you could possibly love me back. Not this much, anyway."

He was quiet for a long time, stroking her hair. He was weighing his words like he always did. When the suspense was about to do her in, he finally leaned down and kissed the crown of her head.

"Welcome to *my* world, Deanna Jackson,"

he whispered, tipping her face up. "Now you know how I've felt for the last seventeen years. I'm sure I'll still be feeling it when I'm eighty."

Then his mouth found hers and he kissed her. It was a powerful kiss. A kiss that left no more room for doubt.

EPILOGUE

One Month Later
Roundup Rodeo, Kinakane, WA

The brightly lit Ridge to River course was lined with spectators who had to stagger their feet to keep from sliding back down the incline they'd just climbed. Sean stood atop Suicide Hill, fueling himself on the crowd's excitement. He could hear the carnival goers' squeals and the crashing waves of cheers rising up from the arena below. Were they cheering for Deanna yet? Her other horse, Star, had been confiscated along with the rest of Blake's possessions. She was riding Sean's stallion tonight, whom she'd finally given a name: Firestorm. As heartbreaking as it was for her to lose Star, Firestorm and Deanna were an unbeatable duo. Sean pitied her competition.

He could also hear the drums lifting uphill from the Native American encampment. Closing his eyes, he savored the coursing connection with his people. Most of the riders up here raced because of that very feeling. They risked themselves and their horses because participating in tradition was an honor and a way to pass something important to new generations. That same conviction ran deep in Sean, too. It was why he hoped his own sons would do this someday.

But as the Ferris wheel lights winked up at him, he knew that tonight it held other meaning, as well. This race marked a new beginning and a new Sean. He'd been stalled for too long, avoiding risk to protect himself. Tonight would be a symbolic leap of faith.

Sean's mustang, Boaz, reared, straining against the reins, its eyes wild. It didn't appreciate being held back at all.

A jockey behind him let out a joyful call to battle that was echoed by the others. Sean grinned. They were working up adrenaline.

And guts.

Sean needed some of that, too. "You play it too safe," Deanna had told him after a practice earlier this week. "You've got to quit holding back."

Boaz tugged, whinnying.

"Soon. We've got to wait for Deanna to win first."

Sean wished he could watch her. "Go, Deanna,

go," he whispered as he swung up onto Boaz's back. He could see the whole valley stretching below him, where the sun had dipped behind the western horizon—nothing more now than a fiery glow of red and gold melting into twilight.

The fires wouldn't be completely out until winter's snow extinguished them, but they were mostly contained and were no longer a threat to Kinakane or to his ranch. The winds had cleared the smoke away and everyone seemed to be breathing easier now.

Not many people had escaped without scars, though.

Sean thought of his own scars. They went much deeper than the charred acres on his property or the cost of the livestock he'd lost.

There were scars of betrayal and grief that would take more than a handful of weeks to heal. But just as the green shoots of regrowth would burst through the burnt ground soon, healing would come to these places inside him, too. He knew it was true. A wave of bittersweet conviction rolled over him. He would no longer be defined by his losses.

He pumped his fist into the air and let loose a loud, powerful war cry of his own before he lined up at the start line, fifty feet back from the edge of the cliff. Cheers and more cries rang out from the men beside him. Sean tightened the strap on his helmet and life jacket. There was nothing left to do but listen to Bo's heaving and wait for the signal.

"This is for you, Dad," Sean yelled into the night.

Then the starting pistol cracked and they were off, sprinting to the edge. Sean was the first one to crest it. He rode straight downhill through a tangle of men and horses, of dust and spitting rocks. They raced to the soundtrack of pounding hooves, the shouts of the riders and the call of the crowd below them beckoning them into the arena.

As they crashed into the river at the bottom, Sean hardly felt the cold, wet spray or his soaked pant legs. He leaned forward, hollering encouragement into Bo's ear as the horse swam. They had only seconds to take the lead.

"Come on, Bo! We've got this!"

They exited the river at the same moment the palomino beside them did, putting them neck and neck, scrambling and fighting their way up the embankment. Only five hundred feet separated them from the finish line. The vision of Deanna on Firestorm played across Sean's mind. She wouldn't accept defeat and neither would he.

"Win!" Sean cried.

They ran through the arena doors, the two

glistening horses side by side. Sean rocked forward, flattening himself against Bo's neck to reach for the goal. He could see the orange finish-line flags, was vaguely aware of the people jumping up and down cheering them on.

One last burst of energy from Bo and then it was over.

"And Boaz ridden by his owner, Sean Loomis, comes in first by a nose. Next we have..." But Sean didn't hear the rest of the riders' names. The cheering was almost as deafening as the roar inside his own head.

Then he caught a flash of white-blond hair in his periphery. Deanna stood by the arena gate, hollering his name, her grin so brilliant it almost knocked him off his horse. Almost made him doubt what he had to do next.

Kicking Boaz forward, Sean thundered to Deanna's side. He reached out a hand to her, smiling at the absolute shock on her face.

"What are you doing?" she laughed.

"Get on," he demanded. "You're doing the victory lap with me."

She grabbed his hand and swung on behind him. The crowd ate it up as they circled the arena. Deanna had one arm wrapped around his waist and used her other hand to salute the crowd with the traditional rodeo-queen wave.

"I didn't know you had this kind of show-manship in you, Loomis," Deanna yelled.

"I'm not done yet," he called back.

"Looks like we've got ourselves a double treat," the velvet voice of the announcer said. "Our Ridge to River victor has kidnapped our barrel-racing champ. Ladies and gentlemen, why don't you put your hands together and let these two winners know how much you appreciate them."

The crowd responded, clapping and stomping the bleachers until their lap ended. Sean aimed Bo for the arena's center, slowing only enough to hop off in a jog.

"What's this? It doesn't seem like Loomis is done, yet," said the announcer, amused. "Whatcha doin', cowboy?"

Sean faced Deanna and offered her his hand again.

"What *are* you doing, cowboy?" she asked, hopping down beside him.

Sean dropped the reins and slapped the horse's backside. Boaz galloped away as Sean took a knee.

There was a collective intake of breath from the stands. Deanna gasped and clutched her clasped hands to her mouth. Tears welled in her gray eyes, making them look greener than ever.

"Deanna," Sean said in a voice that only she

could hear. "I have loved you my whole life. I can't promise I'll do this right, but if you'll let me, I'll die trying."

He swallowed the lump in his throat and said, "Will you marry me?"

Deanna blinked rapidly, unable to find her voice. He watched the emotion dance across her face. She couldn't speak, but she nodded her head vigorously and pulled him to his feet. She almost knocked him over as she jumped into his arms and buried her face in his neck.

"Ladies and gents, I don't know about you, but that looks to me like a yes!" cried the announcer.

The crowd went wild, and Deanna found her voice.

"Yes," she whispered. Then she threw her hat high into the air and whooped, "Yes! Yes! Yes! A hundred times, yes!"

* * * * *

Dear Reader,

Thank you for reading this story. I celebrated with Deanna as she learned that trusting God made her stronger not weaker, and ached for Sean as he faced such deep betrayal and loss. I hope you were rooting for them as much as I was and that they earned a tender place in your heart.

This book was the most challenging story I've written to date. I felt a huge pressure to get it right because I wanted it to be a love letter to a place that is dear to me. The fictional town of Kinakane was inspired by the small towns of Okanogan County in North Central Washington State where my family calls home. I know I didn't do it justice, but I hope I somehow conveyed a small taste of the rich culture, the amazing strength of the people who live there and the rugged, high desert beauty that make the Okanogan Valley so striking. You can visit my Crash Landing board on Pinterest to see more.

I love to hear from readers. You can find me online on Twitter (@BeckyAvella) and my "Becky Avella, author" Facebook page. I look forward to connecting with you.

May God bless you,
Becky Avella

Get 2 Free Books,
Plus 2 Free Gifts—
just for trying the Reader Service!

Get 2 Free Books,
Plus 2 Free Gifts—
just for trying the Reader Service!

♥ HARLEQUIN
HEARTWARMING™

HW17

HOMETOWN HEARTS ♥

YES! Please send me **The Hometown Hearts Collection** in Larger Print. This collection begins with 3 FREE books and 2 FREE gifts in the first shipment. Along with my 3 free books, I'll also get the next 4 books from the Hometown Hearts Collection, in LARGER PRINT, which I may either return and owe nothing, or keep for the low price of $4.99 U.S./ $5.89 CDN each plus $2.99 for shipping and handling per shipment*. If I decide to continue, about once a month for 8 months I will get 6 or 7 more books, but will only need to pay for 4. That means 2 or 3 books in every shipment will be FREE! If I decide to keep the entire collection, I'll have paid for only 32 books because 19 books are FREE! I understand that accepting the 3 free books and gifts places me under no obligation to buy anything. I can always return a shipment and cancel at any time. My free books and gifts are mine to keep no matter what I decide.

262 HCN 3432 462 HCN 3432

Name	(PLEASE PRINT)

Address	Apt. #

City	State/Prov.	Zip/Postal Code

Signature (if under 18, a parent or guardian must sign)

Mail to the **Reader Service:**

IN U.S.A.: P.O. Box 1867, Buffalo, NY. 14240-1867
IN CANADA: P.O. Box 609, Fort Erie, Ontario L2A 5X3

READERSERVICE.COM

Manage your account online!

- Review your order history
- Manage your payments
- Update your address

*We've designed the
Reader Service website
just for you.*

Enjoy all the features!

- Discover new series available to you, and read excerpts from any series.
- Respond to mailings and special monthly offers.
- Browse the Bonus Bucks catalog and online-only exculsives.
- Share your feedback.

Visit us at:
ReaderService.com

RS16R